Dear Readers,

Trust Me On This, originally published in 1997, is the only screwball comedy I've ever written. Wikipedia says that screwball comedy is " a combination of slapstick with fast-paced repartee, and a plot involving courtship and marriage [and] mistaken identities or other circumstances in which a character or characters try to keep some important fact a secret." Yep, that's *Trust Me On This*. Doors are slammed, identities are mistaken, drinks are spilled along with secrets, and everybody has an angle. Writing it made me feel like that guy who used to spin plates on TV: I had so many story lines rotating frantically in the air that it was a miracle nothing broke. But like in any good screwball comedy, the heart of the story is the romance, and that was solid and sure. Dennie and Alec may not have planned on each other or on any of the other things that go so wrong during one fast-paced weekend, but they're good at adapting and even better at falling in love. I had so much fun spinning those plates in *Trust Me On This*, and now I'm hoping you'll have as much fun reading it.

Jenny Crusie

Jenny Crusie

Bantam Books by Jennifer Crusie

The Cinderella Deal
Trust Me on This

JENNIFER CRUSIE

Trust Me on This

BANTAM BOOKS
NEW YORK

2010 Bantam Books Mass Market Edition

Copyright © 1997 by Jennifer Crusie

Published in the United States by Bantam Books, an imprint of The Random House Publishing Group, a division of Random House, Inc., New York.

BANTAM BOOKS and the rooster colophon are registered trademarks of Random House, Inc.

Originally published in hardcover in the United States by Bantam Books, an imprint of The Random House Publishing Group, a division of Random House, Inc., in 1997.

ISBN 978-0-553-59338-9

Cover illustration: Anne Keenan Higgins

Printed in the United States of America

www.bantamdell.com

6 8 9 7 5

*For Ruth Flinn Smith,
sweet, smart, funny, kind, loyal, and loving,
my sister-in-law who became my sister,
and the best present my brother ever gave me*

Trust Me
on This

Chapter 1

Four Fabulous Days!
Three Glorious Nights!
Join the 4th Annual Popular
Literature Conference at the
Historic Riverbend Queen Hotel!!!
April 7, 8, 9, & 10
Your Life Will Never Be the Same!!!

Victoria Prentice found the card as she sorted through her mail and stood transfixed by the tackiness of it. It wasn't the first time she'd been disgusted by academic stupidity in the forty years she'd been teaching college students, but it was the first time she'd been both disgusted and involved. She'd agreed to deliver a paper at this circus so she could spend some time with her friend Janice, but she wouldn't have if she'd known that this was how they were going to publicize it. The card promised everything except live girls and free drinks. Well, there went her reputation as a scholar. What were the idiots thinking of? It was all very well to take a stand against academic rigidity, but shilling a lit conference as if it were Club Med—

She stopped, appalled by the fussiness of her own thoughts. A lifetime of independence and freethinking, and what did she have to show for it? She was sixty-two years old and petrifying as she stood there. *I'm getting old,* she thought. *Old in mind. That's a terrible thing.* She'd spent too much of her life arguing over dead authors and dead literature, playing it safe, and now she was sneering at something lively. Getting smug. Isolated. Victoria felt a twinge of something like dissatisfaction and shrugged it off.

She was not dissatisfied. She'd worked damn hard to get where she was, and she'd loved every minute of it. No, her life was fine, she just needed a jump start, a change of pace, to be with somebody who would jolt her out of her rut. Janice was all very well, but she was also happily married and stable as the earth. Victoria needed to be with somebody alive, somebody young, somebody like her nephew.

Exactly like her nephew.

Alec wasn't an infant, of course. She counted back. She was twenty-four years older than he was so . . . good Lord, he was thirty-eight. How had that happened? While she was slowly turning to rock, he'd been aging too. Well, it didn't matter. He was still younger than she was, still able to make her feel alive when she was with him.

I'm not ready to solidify yet, she thought. Alec would go to the conference with her. He always did whatever she asked since she never asked much, and once there, she could bicker with him over dinner and harass him about settling down before he hit forty, and generally use him to get an attitude adjustment while she watched him dazzle every woman in the place with his aw-shucks charm and farm-boy face. If her life was dull and stuffy and essentially over, at least she still had the energy to interfere in his. She fed the card into the fax machine and punched in his office fax number, and when it went through, she picked up her phone and dialed him.

"I just faxed you an invitation for a month from now," she told him when he picked up the phone. "Accept it or you'll rot in hell for disappointing your favorite relative who gave you the best summers of your life."

"I accept," Alec said. "And hello to you too."

Alec Prentice tossed the fax on his boss's desk. "Three glorious nights, Harry. That's what we both need."

Harry Chase grunted and tossed it back, refusing to move his eyes from his computer.

"No, Harry." Alec put the paper in front of the older man again. "Look at it."

Harry glanced at it. "Great." He stared back into the computer screen.

"That's where I'm going next month. My aunt's speaking at this conference, and I'm going." Alec waited and then said, "Harry, I'm going out of town three weeks from Thursday. Hello?"

"I know." Harry ducked his grizzled head as he clicked a couple of keys. The computer screen flexed and rearranged itself, and Harry growled at it.

"Harry—" Alec tried again.

"I *know*." Harry looked up from the screen. "You're going to hear your aunt give a speech. You told me. I know." His eyes shifted back to the screen.

"It's a literature conference, Harry," Alec said distinctly. "College professors."

Harry's eyes stayed on the screen. "So?"

"I was thinking of that guy who came up on the scan the other day, Brian Bond. He's never pulled his con in Ohio, and he's running out of states."

Harry took his gaze from the screen and narrowed his eyes at Alec.

"Right." Alec relaxed now that he had Harry's attention. "This is a nice convention. According to my aunt, nobody's reputation ever got made or unmade at a pop lit conference. They'll all be rested, optimistic, and probably juiced. It's prime stuff for Bond."

Harry considered it, shrugged, and turned back to the computer. "It's a long shot."

"What's wrong with you?" Alec surveyed the older man with disgust. "You used to be the first one on the trail. I know you've got twenty years on me, but you can't be giving up yet. Two years in front of a computer and all of a sudden you're not interested in actually nailing the bad guys?"

"It's a long shot," Harry repeated. "The database isn't."

"There is more to life than a national database," Alec said.

"Not to my life," Harry said.

"Well, I wouldn't brag about it." Alec retrieved the announcement. "Bond usually works with a woman, right?"

Harry punched a couple of keys, and the screen rescrambled itself. "Right," he said as he read the profile. "A brunette. We don't have much on her. His last hit was in Nashville, three months ago."

"Maybe she'll seduce me," Alec said hopefully.

"I'll wear my glasses. It's amazing how many people try to sell me things when I wear my glasses."

Harry snorted again and Alec knew why: It wasn't amazing at all, it was a calculated effect. He thought wistfully of how in the past he'd traded on his open face to perfect a doofus persona that included horn-rimmed glasses, a slightly vacant look in his eyes, and a smile reminiscent of an overeager junior high kid. Con men had rushed to sign him up. He'd bought lakefront property, oceanfront property, exciting stocks, miraculous bonds, and, shortly after that, the con men had gone to jail while Alec smiled blankly at them.

It had been a great job, he thought now with some regret. He'd set his own hours and annoyed the hell out of self-important people who cheated little old ladies for a living. And then, just when he was becoming so well-known that it was getting difficult to convince cons to sell him chewing gum let alone phantom real estate, Harry had plucked him out of the field to work on his pet project, the Federal Fraud Database. It was important work and Alec was dedicated to it, but he missed the thrill of the hunt. He was solidifying behind a computer, turning into Harry Chase before his time. He needed to break out again, pit his wits against somebody agile and evil just one more time before he went back to being Harry's computer heir apparent forever.

And that's how long he was going to be heir apparent because Harry was never going to retire. Alec examined that thought, a little surprised at the impatience behind it. He liked Harry. More than that, he respected him and was grateful to him. Harry had done a hell of a lot for him, pushed him for promotion, made sure he was in the right places at the right times, attached him to the new database project. He was Harry's protégé and damn lucky to be so.

He just missed running his own show.

Maybe that was why he missed the field. He didn't miss the endless hotels and the bad food and the lousy people and the lying. He missed calling the shots.

Well, maybe Bond would show up in Riverbend and he'd get to call the shots one more time. He went back to the thrill of pitting his wits again. If the someone agile and evil he was pitting against was also female, attractive, and immoral, so much the better. He'd been working too hard and dating too little. "I need a furlough, Harry," Alec said, and Harry snorted.

"Dream on," he said. "Go baby-sit your aunt. But call me if Bond turns up. I'll need to put it in the computer. And let me know if he's working with that woman too. And get her name. We need the data."

"She's a brunette," Alec said to no one in particular. "I wouldn't mind being seduced by a brunette." He looked down at the fax again. "I could use three glorious nights too. Hell, I'd settle for one glorious night."

Harry snorted again, and Alec ignored him and went back to fantasizing about succumbing to a dark-haired con woman in the line of duty three weeks from Thursday.

Two weeks later and two states away, Dennie Banks shoved her dark curls back from her face so she could glare at her editor unimpeded. "It's just three nights, a week from now, Taylor," she told him as he frowned over the "Four Fabulous Days" announcement card. "It's my weekend. I just need next Friday off."

"What if something happens on Friday?" Taylor's weasely little eyes squinted up at her.

"Like what? An emergency wedding?" Dennie tried to keep the exasperation out of her voice. "I write for lifestyles and the women's page. There is no late-breaking news on the women's page."

"You never know," Taylor said portentously, and Dennie knew there was absolutely no thought behind the statement. It was Taylor's version of "because I said so." Most of the time, Taylor's brain-deadness did not bother her; in fact, it was one of the reasons she'd stayed working for him for twelve years. She knew Taylor, she could handle Taylor, so she stayed with Taylor.

Lately, though, that sameness bothered her, and the bother made her voice firmer than usual. "I'm flying out next Thursday, Taylor. You won't need me."

"All right, Banks," he growled. "But if anything happens, you better get your tail back here."

"You bet," Dennie said, and left the office

annoyed and unsettled. She plopped into her desk chair and leaned back, and then her annoyance evaporated and she smiled at the woman who had just arrived in the newsroom.

"I'm sorry." Patience tossed her purse on her desk. "I shouldn't have said any of that stuff last night. It was none of my business."

"No, I'm glad you did." Dennie took a deep breath. "I thought about it all night, and you're right. The most exciting thing in my life is Walter. And Walter's a Yorkie."

"Look, I'm right about *my* life." Patience dropped into her desk chair. "I couldn't take dating those safe boring guys you have twisted around your finger—"

"I know," Dennie said.

"—or reporting on the same damn stuff every day even if you are the best in the world at it—"

"I know," Dennie said.

"—or working for Taylor for twelve years, and how you've stood *that,* I'll never know—"

"Patience, I know," Dennie said. "We had this discussion last night."

11

"—but you're not living my life," Patience finished. "So who am I to judge?"

"My best friend for my whole life?" Dennie said. "That's somebody to judge. And you're right. I thought about it, and you're right. But I can't change bosses, men, and careers at the same time, so I decided to focus on one."

"Oh, thank God," Patience said, sinking back in her chair. "You're quitting here and leaving Taylor behind."

"Well, no," Dennie said. "I need things like rent and health insurance. I have to stay with Taylor for a while. And I can't handle dating complicated men right now, so I'm just going to give men up entirely until I get the career thing under control. That's where I'm making my change." Dennie leaned forward and Patience did, too, until their heads were as close as the desks between them would allow. "I have a lead on this story." Dennie glanced over her shoulder, but no one in the room was paying them any attention. "Janice Severs Meredith is speaking at the Popular Literature Conference in Riverbend next weekend."

"Who's Janice Severs Meredith? No, wait."

Patience held up her hand. "Janice Meredith. She wrote *The Feminist Marriage,* right? And *Redefining Relationships*? I heard her speak once. She's brilliant."

"She's also getting a divorce," Dennie said, and Patience gaped. "I know. I found out about it last week. It's still very hush-hush, but it's due to break anytime now. And I want the interview."

"How did you find out?"

"I was interviewing this writer who was in town doing a book signing. Twenty, beautiful, but with the brain of a cranberry. She writes about the depth of angst in the twenty-something set." Dennie rolled her eyes. "She wouldn't know angst if it bit her. Anyway, I was getting nowhere with her, so I asked her about the writers who had inspired her, and she said that her future husband was her biggest influence and her biggest admirer. So I said, 'Future husband?' and she said, 'Yes,' and he was very intellectual because he had two books on *The New York Times* bestseller list right now."

"Charles Meredith," Patience said.

"Well, that's what I said, and then she frowned

and said that I couldn't say anything because he hadn't told his wife yet."

"Ouch."

Dennie nodded. "Like I said, the brains of a cranberry. And evidently the morals of a mink. So now all I have to do is track Janice Meredith down."

"And drop this bomb on her?" Patience looked horrified. "You wouldn't."

"No, of course I wouldn't," Dennie said. "He must have told her by now, especially since Tallie dropped the bomb on me."

"Tallie?"

"The future Mrs. Meredith. I promise, I'll be careful not to hurt her. But"—Dennie swallowed—"I'm going to get this story. You were right. I've been stagnating, only writing inconsequential stories because I didn't have to go after them, because I was afraid I'd fail. This one is important, and it's going to be tough, but I'm getting it."

Patience looked as if she had reservations. "So you're just going to walk right up to her and say, 'So, Janice, about this divorce?' "

"No, of course not." Dennie frowned. "That would be cruel and I don't want to hurt her, she's going through enough. But she's had such a huge impact on modern marriage, and what she has to say about divorce is going to be even more important. And I want to be the one who does the first interview where she talks about it. With that interview"—Dennie glanced over her shoulder again—"I can get out of here and into the big leagues. One step at a time. I know you wanted me revolutionizing my life, but I can't afford—"

"I think this is great," Patience said. "I think you're doing the smartest thing possible. I'll even dog-sit Walter."

Dennie felt the muscles in her neck relax for the first time since the night before when Patience had tackled her about her too safe life. Patience had stood in the middle of the tissue-papered aftermath of her bridal shower and said, "Dennie, it's time you moved on too," and the argument that followed hadn't been their first, but it had been their worst. "You're getting by on your charm, Dennie," Patience had said. "You're not even using your brains. Go after life and stop sitting around waiting for it to come to you." Dennie had been so insulted, she'd stomped out, but after a sleepless night, she knew she hadn't been insulted, she'd been terrified. She'd been afraid, holding on to a safe life that wasn't giving her what she needed, and now that she was taking steps to break away, she could feel the relief in her bones. "I wouldn't have done this without you," she told Patience. "Although I still can't believe you're deserting me to get married and move to New York. How could you?"

Patience relaxed back into her chair. "He sleeps with me. You don't."

"Walter sleeps with me," Dennie said. "Although I suppose it's not the same. How am I going to survive without you around to pick me up when I fall?"

"Don't fall," Patience said. "Or better yet, learn to pick yourself up. You underestimate yourself all the time, Dennie. You can do the tough stuff, and you can do it on your own. You just have to believe."

"Right," Dennie said. "Believe. Piece of cake."

* * *

"Don't tell me it's a piece of cake," the brunette told her partner one week later. "We've been pushing our luck too long. This isn't going to work. We have to get out. *Please*."

Brian Bond rolled his eyes at the ceiling. "Sherée, I told you, this time it's foolproof. This time, it's *legal*. We can't lose."

"No," Sherée said. "I have a really bad feeling about this. I don't think we should go." She fidgeted a little, bending the card in her hand back and forth.

Bond checked his watch to show her how impatient he was. He didn't really need to check because he always knew what time it was; success was in the details. "We have exactly forty-six minutes to catch the plane for Riverbend," he told her. "We are going. Move it."

"Did you hear me?" she asked. "Do you ever hear me? We're going to get caught. We've got to stop this."

"Can we have this argument on the plane?" Bond tested the lock on his suitcase one last time.

"You know you're going. You've gotten cold feet before and you've gone, so why even bother talking about it? Now get your bag. We're out of here."

"No, we're not." Sherée picked the announcement card up from the table. "You know your 'Four Fabulous Days!'? Well, watch this." She tore the card in half. "That's you and me," she told Bond, her voice quavering. "I'm out of here. You go and get caught. I'm staying out of jail."

She picked up her bag and walked out the door, and Bond watched her go with some surprise. He'd had no idea Sherée had any backbone at all. Not that it mattered. He could do this one just as well without her. After six months, she'd become a pain in the butt, always needing reassurance, always looking over her shoulder, always looking *guilty*. Some women just weren't cut out for crime.

He checked the mirror on his way out the door, smiling his best honest smile. He looked as if guilt never crossed his mind. It didn't. "Trust me," he said to the mirror, and the mirror beamed back the

face of a towheaded farm boy, right out of Nor-
man Rockwell.

Brian Bond laughed all the way to the airport.

Sherée had turned in her plane ticket for Riverbend at the airport counter, consoling herself that
the hefty amount of money she'd lost on the exchange was really Brian's since he'd paid for the
ticket originally. It wasn't much consolation, and
the loss of the money coupled with the fact that
she hadn't a clue what to do next made her depressed, and she didn't like being depressed. If she
wasn't happy, it must be somebody else's fault,
and that somebody else must be Brian who should
have been taking care of her, and he really should
be sorry about that, but she was pretty sure he
wasn't. This was so depressing, Sherée sat in the
airport bar and stewed about it for a while.

Eventually she noticed that this was not helping her situation in the slightest, and then she
began to plan, a new experience for her. Walking
out had been a good idea only as a threat, she realized. Taking care of herself held absolutely no

interest at all for her. She was going to have to find Brian again and convince him to take care of her until she could find somebody else who could do the job better. It was stupid of her to have walked away without having another man to walk away to. Her only problem was, Brian was in Riverbend by now.

She should never have cashed in that plane ticket. It just went to show you, somebody else should have been there making the decisions.

Three hours later, Sherée got on the bus for Riverbend. By now Brian would have seen how wrong he was and be ready to apologize, or she'd make sure he was when she got there. Either way, at least she was doing something. Sherée leaned her head on the window and went to sleep, dreaming of validation and vengeance.

Chapter 2

Dennie went flying through the brass-framed revolving doors of the Riverbend Queen Hotel, her cheeks glowing from the April wind, and plowed right into a handsome, lanky blond in the middle of the red-flocked hotel lobby.

"I'm *so* sorry," she said, and he smiled at her, a shy smile that might have warmed her heart if she hadn't just given up men for the duration. He looked like her type: easy to enslave.

"That's all right," he said. "It was my fault. Not lookin' where I was goin'." He stuck out his hand. "I'm Brian Bondman. Pleased to meet you."

Dennie shook his hand once. "My pleasure." She turned to go, but he held on.

"You sure are a pretty sight comin' through that door—" he began.

Dennie tugged her hand back. "Thank you." She turned to go again, but he'd sidled around her so she was face-to-face with him.

"I sure would be willin' to take you to dinner tonight to make up for this," he said and ducked his head at his own temerity.

This is an act, Dennie told herself. *Nobody drops that many g's naturally.* It would be interesting to know why it was an act, but not very. "No," she said, and pulled her hand away. "But thank you anyway." Then she turned and headed for the brass-edged registration desk before he could leap in front of her and offer drinks, frozen yogurt, or breakfast. He had the look of a man who didn't quit trying, all that aw shucks to the contrary.

"I have a reservation," she told the registration clerk. "Dennie Banks?"

The clerk took her form when she'd signed it,

handed her the key card to her room, and said, "Is there anything else?"

This was it. *Don't waste a minute,* she told herself. Dennie leaned forward. "Yes, I'm supposed to meet Janice Meredith here. Do you know——?"

"She's in the Ivy Room," the clerk said. "Right over there beyond the bar."

"Could you hold my bag for me, please?" Dennie passed her carry-on over the desk. "I don't want to miss her."

Be firm, she told herself as she headed for the restaurant. *Be professional and firm and focused. Believe in yourself.*

Right.

Alec had taken it all in from his well-upholstered seat in the mahogany and brass hotel bar, and he'd never been more delighted to see a hunch pay off. He'd been watching Bond case the lobby when the brunette had started up the steps to the revolving door. Bond saw her at the same time and moved to meet her, deliberately running into her as she came through the doors, and Alec thought, *Nice touch. Anybody seeing them would swear it was an accident.* The brunette had smiled at him and moved away almost immediately, but Alec knew they'd spoken. Bond had even faked disappointment as she'd walked away.

Watching the brunette now, Alec sympathized with Bond; it wouldn't be hard faking disappointment if this woman walked away from you. Glossy dark brown curls bounced on her shoulders, and her smile heated the lobby. She walked past him to the registration desk, and he watched her hips move under her fluid red dress. She had a great swing to her.

Normally he'd wait until the con approached him; it was safer, less suspicious, but this was a woman any man would approach. In fact, he told himself, it would be more suspicious if he *didn't* approach her, and the last thing he wanted was to be more suspicious. So when she handed her bag to the clerk and turned toward the restaurant next to the bar, he moved to meet her, just like any red-blooded American man in his right, if gullible, mind would do.

"Are you all right, ma'am?" he asked. "You hit that guy pretty hard."

She smiled briefly and stepped away, turning toward the restaurant, her red skirt flaring around her very nice calves. "I'm fine, thank you."

"You might want a brandy." Alec eased himself alongside her. "It would be my privilege to buy you one. I'm a stranger here myself, but I do know how to buy a pretty lady a brandy."

She stopped and her eyes got narrower. "Is there some kind of convention here besides pop literature? Some farm-boy thing?"

"I don't know." Alec tried to look open and eager to please. "I could sure find out. I'm all alone here, got plenty of time, and it would be a real act of kindness if you'd join me." The woman opened her mouth to protest and he finished, "Now don't you worry about a thing. I got plenty of money and I'd just love to spend it on you. Would you like—?"

"No," she said, moving away from him again. "I wouldn't like anything you could give me. Thank you anyway."

She disappeared into the restaurant and Alec

watched her go, still wincing a little from the "anything you could give me" line. Better marks than he were evidently having brunch. He gave her a couple of minutes and then trailed in after her, taking a table across the room where he could watch her without seeming to.

As soon as he sat down, he knew he was in trouble. She was there all right, but sitting in the booth next to her were his aunt Victoria and two of her friends, all of whom had known him since babyhood. All he needed was for one of them to spot him across the room and start yodeling hellos, and his cover would be history. He sidled out again, but not before he noticed the brunette was eavesdropping on them.

Five minutes later, Harry picked up the phone and said, "What?"

"Harry, that's a lousy way to answer the phone," Alec said. "You've still got seven years to go until retirement. Try a little polish, a little sophistication."

"At two-thirty in the afternoon, when all hell is breaking loose, and you're sitting on your butt in Ohio instead of here where you belong, you get

'What?'," Harry growled. "You want me polished and sophisticated, you call another time."

"If I want you polished and sophisticated, I'll have to call another planet."

"You calling to resign?"

"Hell no," Alec said cheerfully. "Somebody's got to help you out, old man. Guess who I just saw?"

Harry snorted. "A blonde."

"Yep. And this blond you're interested in. Brian Bond."

"You're kidding." Harry sounded dumbfounded. "He's really there?"

"Oh, yes. The Shadow always knows, Harry. You never trust me."

Harry snorted. "What about the woman?"

"Oh, she's here too." Alec grinned. "A very hot brunette. She blew me off when I tried to be the greatest mark God ever sent her. Not too swift obviously, but then she's quite a looker. He probably doesn't keep her around for her brains."

"This is too good to be true," Harry said. "I love it. Make your move on the brunette. Try to convince her to sell you something."

Alec thought about making his move on the brunette, and his pulse kicked up. "The sacrifices I make for you. If necessary, I'll even let her drag me to bed. Anything else?"

"Yeah, I want you to go after Bond directly too. It would help if we could nail him in the act." There was a long silence, and Alec waited patiently. "You know any college professors?" Harry asked finally.

"I was hoping you'd ask," Alec said. "My aunt Victoria is brave, honest, intelligent, unpredictable, and here. And the good news is, the brunette is already scoping her out. We won't even have to plant her; they're already on her scent."

"Unpredictable is bad," Harry growled. "Not that all women aren't. Don't you know any guy professors?"

Alec frowned at the phone. "Hell, Harry, I just gave you a perfectly good professor who's already a mark. You want a custom job, get one yourself."

"I better go there," Harry said. "I'll fly out tonight. Keep your eyes open, and concentrate on the woman until I get there."

"No problem," Alec said. "She is definitely worth concentrating on."

The Ivy Room was a restaurant, Dennie found out, and the walls dividing the room from the lobby and the booths from one another were open brass lattice woven with brass ivy leaves. Janice Meredith hadn't been hard to spot as the place was almost deserted in the middle of the afternoon. Dennie slid into the next booth and watched out of the corner of her eye through the lattice as the three women talked.

One was a dumpy little grandmother with a full head of tight blue curls; one was a white-haired, bright-eyed, midsized dynamo; and one—the one with her back to Dennie—was a regal presence, her hair styled in an elegant black razor cut feathered with white. They were all wearing expensive suits and expensive perfume, and they all looked like success. The only one Dennie recognized was the one with the razor cut. Janice Meredith.

"Are you really all right, Janice?" the dynamo was saying. "Don't be a martyr with us."

"Victoria, I am not now nor have I ever been a martyr," Janice Meredith said. "I've been better, but I'm doing fine. My marriage died, not my child."

"That's very true," the blue-haired woman said. "How is Maggie?"

"I know it's just your marriage, but it still hurts," Victoria said. "I remember."

"Well, hurt is better than no feeling at all," Janice said. "In a way, this is good. I think I was having it all too easy."

"And Charles, Junior? How is Charles, Junior?" the blue-haired one went on.

"Never mind that, Trella," Victoria said. "This is serious. Now listen to me, Janice, if you're going to say something about this as a growth experience, you can forget it. Women our age don't need growth experiences."

"Oh, yes, we do," Janice said. "We need to keep taking chances, or we stagnate. Especially women our age. I don't think this divorce is my fault—"

"Good," Victoria muttered.

"Just one of those things," Trella murmured aimlessly.

"—but I don't think I was doing much to save my marriage, either. I was comfortable. So I didn't pay attention."

"This is not your fault," Victoria began, outrage in her voice.

"So this is really good for me," Janice went on serenely. "It's my wake-up call. I've only been doing the easy things. I've been in a rut. I need to take some risks, fail a little. I really believe that if you're not failing now and then, you're not trying hard enough. Failure says, well, at least you're living. You're stretching." She cocked her head at Victoria. "I'm planning on doing a lot more failing in the future. And a hell of a lot more succeeding too. I'll be fine."

"The worst thing about being your friend is constantly feeling inferior to you," Victoria said. "You're right, of course, but isn't there at least a tiny little part of you that wants to castrate Charles Meredith with a dull spoon?"

"Victoria, really," Trella said.

"Why don't we change the subject?" Janice

said, patting Trella's hand. "How are the grand-children, Trella?"

Dennie sank back away from the lattice and stared into space. *That's my interview,* she thought. She could hang the whole thing on the risking quote. Any other woman might bend under the weight of what Janice Meredith was going through, but she was going to go out and risk it all again. She was incredible. Patience would love her. Well, from now on Dennie was risking too.

And she was going to start with the biggest risk of all: She was going to approach Janice Meredith.

She waited until the three got up and parted company at the door of the restaurant, and then she followed her quarry to the elevator. Dennie jammed her hand in the closing doors and slid through the opening, smiling her best Hi-tell-me-about-your-wedding smile at the startled woman.

"Professor Meredith," she said, holding out her hand. "I'm Dennie Banks, and I'm so pleased to meet you. I've enjoyed your work so much."

"Thank you." Janice Meredith took her hand cautiously and dropped it almost immediately.

"That's why I'd like to interview you," Dennie said. "I couldn't help but overhear you at lunch today—"

The woman's cool reserve froze immediately into iceberg disgust.

"—and I think what you said is terribly important," Dennie said hurriedly. "I think you have an important message for women in your position—"

The woman took a step back, and Dennie speeded up even more.

"—and I would be *honored* to be the writer who—"

"Miss Banks," Janice Meredith said coldly. "If I want a message sent, *I* will be the one to send it. And I might add, reputable journalists do not get their stories through eavesdropping."

"No, no," Dennie said, waving her hands. "I had the story before. I was looking for you. I came to this conference specifically to see you. To interview you about this."

She stopped because the woman's face had gone white. "It's out then," she whispered to herself. "Everybody knows."

"No, no," Dennie said again, frantically this

time. "I only found out because I interviewed Tallie Gamble and—"

"And you want to do a comparison interview with the two of us?" The iceberg suddenly flared into a propane torch. "No. Not while I have breath, do you understand?"

"No, that's not it—" Dennie began, but the elevator doors were open, and Janice Meredith stormed out, her rage making her deaf to any argument.

Dennie leaned back in the elevator and closed her eyes.

Not good. She felt her panic rise and told herself to stay calm. This was what risking was all about. It was a setback, not a failure. All she had to do was analyze what she'd done wrong.

Well, first, she'd been dumb. She was used to people who *wanted* to talk to her, who were dying to describe the centerpieces at their anniversary parties. She should have been more convincing. Second, she should have known that the serenity Janice Meredith had shown in the restaurant was at least partly a cover for her pain. She should have been more careful. And approaching her in the elevator, that had been stupid too. *Think from now on,* she told herself.

All right. She was going to have to wait until the woman had calmed down before she could even hope to approach her, and even then it was going to be tough. Somehow, she had to convince her of her sincerity. Somehow, she had to show Janice Meredith that she was a reputable journalist, a sympathetic ear. Of course the woman wouldn't talk to just anybody about this. Even if she was committed to a new life of risking, that didn't mean the wounds from the old life weren't still fresh.

But if a friend approached her . . . If a friend told her that this marvelous journalist wanted to present her side of the story . . . If a friend—

Somehow, she had to get an introduction from somebody Janice Meredith trusted.

There had been two of them in the restaurant. Trella and Victoria. There might be several Victorias in the pop literature program, but Dennie was willing to bet there'd be only one Trella. And while Victoria looked sharp, Trella had been only marginally sentient, much like the two guys who'd tried to pick her up in the lobby. Trella was the one to go for.

She punched the button for the lobby and went to pick up her bag and find a program and get her racing heart back under control.

Alec was back sitting in his favorite seat by the brass archway to the bar when the brunette crossed the lobby again. *At last,* he thought. She'd been gone from the restaurant when he'd gotten back from his phone call, and he'd lost her for half an hour. It made him nervous to think of the scores she could have been making while he was looking for her, but she was there now, steaming across the lobby to the phones.

Didn't this woman ever just walk anywhere? Every time he saw her, she was moving full tilt. She'd run Bond into the ground with all that energy. The thought of Bond as recipient of the brunette's energy made him envious. Harry had told him to make a move on her again. It was his duty to draw a little of that energy for himself.

He straightened to go join her, and then

stopped. She was on the phone, checking her watch, and then she hung up and sat down, obviously waiting for someone. Alec relaxed back into his chair to see what she was up to.

Fifteen minutes later, a little blue-haired woman in a silver-gray suit got off the elevator and crossed toward her, and Alec sighed. He knew her, Trella Madison, an old friend of his aunt's, and he also knew she was every con man's dream: friendly, wealthy, and dumb as a rock.

It was starting.

"Thank you for meeting me," Dennie said, sinking into a gilt chair next to Trella. The huge overplush lobby wasn't the best place for an interview—the gold furniture and red-flocked walls made the place look like a nineteenth century Whores "R" Us—but Dennie couldn't afford to be choosy. "You have no idea how much I appreciate this," she told Trella.

"Well, I really just came to tell you that I couldn't possibly talk to you about Janice." Trella beamed at her. "And really, I wish you would just forget this whole thing. You seem like a nice person." She patted Dennie's hand.

"Oh, I *am*." Dennie leaned forward and projected sincerity with every cell in her body. "And I do sympathize with Professor Meredith. Truly, I do. That's why I want to do the interview with her. The press can be savage on something like this." She beamed back at Trella, trying to look intelligent, compassionate, warm, and honest at the same time. It shouldn't have been hard, she felt all of those things, but trying to keep them on her face made her feel like a fraud. "If you could just tell her that I mean only the *best* for her, and I mean the *best*—"

"You know, dear, I think it's a mistake to talk to the press," Trella said, a trifle abstracted. "Sometimes they misquote you, and then sometimes they don't, and you've really said those things, which can be so much worse."

"Don't think of me as the press," Dennie said, trying not to let her intensity flatten the little woman. "Think of me as a friend with a tape recorder. Think of me as somebody who would not dream of misquoting anyone because this is the biggest story of my career, and I want desperately to get everything right."

"I don't think careers like this are good for a woman," Trella said. "They make a woman hard." She tilted her head at Dennie. "You don't look hard yet. Although there is that line between your eyes. Lines are so bad. Why don't you just find a nice man and forget this?" Trella patted Dennie's hand again.

Dennie clenched her teeth and tried to remember that if she ripped Trella's head off, she'd never get the Meredith interview. "Well," she said carefully instead, "don't you think that since I'm not hard yet, that I would be a good person—"

"Miss Banks?"

Dennie jerked her head up at the man's voice. He was a young suit, probably early thirties, painfully thin, prematurely balding and visibly uncomfortable. He was standing beside Janice Meredith.

This could not be good.

"Miss Banks? I'm Paul Baxter, the manager here, and I was wondering if I could see you for a moment?" The man's voice was pleading.

"Why?" Dennie asked, keeping a wary eye on Janice.

"I forgot to tell you, dear," Trella said. "I did call Janice and mention I was meeting you. I hope you don't mind—"

This is bad, Dennie told herself as her heartbeat moved into overdrive. *Nothing I can't handle, but it's bad.*

Janice Meredith broke in. "It's very simple, Miss Banks. I have reported your harassment to Mr. Baxter. If you attempt to question either myself or any of my friends again, I'll have you arrested. Ohio has a stalking law, you know."

"Stalking?" Dennie blinked, confusion goosing her nervousness along. "I'm on your side. Why would I stalk you? If you'd just let me—"

"Trust me, Miss Banks," Janice Meredith said evenly, "I know exactly who is on my side. And you're not even close. Come with me, Trella."

Trella stood up and smiled uncertainly at Dennie. "It was lovely talking to you, dear. Good luck on finding a man."

When they were gone, Dennie realized she was

trembling and clenched her hands together to stop the shaking.

The manager cleared his throat. "I'm sure this was just a misunderstanding," he said, clasping and unclasping his hands. Dennie knew just how he felt. "But if you could avoid Dr. Meredith whenever possible, we'd all be very grateful. And we would like to avoid the police."

"Right," Dennie said. "The police would be bad."

"Thank you," Mr. Baxter said. "I'm sure you meant well, but Dr. Meredith is very powerful, and I just got this promotion, and I—we—the hotel, that is—well, me too—we really can't afford the bad publicity."

"I understand," Dennie said, beginning to feel sorry for him, but sorrier for herself. She'd almost had a heart attack in the ugliest hotel lobby in Ohio.

"The police would probably be bad publicity." Mr. Baxter sounded unsure.

"I'd bet on it," Dennie said.

"Well, then, you understand." Mr. Baxter

nodded once, turned away, turned back, and said, "Uh, enjoy your stay."

"Thank you," Dennie said.

When he was gone, Dennie leaned back for a moment trying to calm her panic-stricken heart. You need to find someone you can't charm, Patience had told her, and then Fate sent her Janice Meredith. What a shame she couldn't call Patience on her honeymoon and tell her; *somebody* should be enjoying this. *Think,* she told herself, and then as she registered the curious looks that passersby were throwing at her as she sat frowning, she shoved herself out of her chair and headed for the mahogany and brass bar she could see through the archway at the end of the lobby. People in bars often scowled at random; she wouldn't be noticeable there.

Once inside the cool darkness, she ordered a scotch from the little redhead behind the bar and contemplated the humiliation of her afternoon. First Janice Meredith had looked at her as if she were lower than Howard Stern. And then there had been Trella, the throwback. Find a nice man, she'd said. And then that wimpy hotel manager who was probably the sole support of a large extended family—

"You okay?" the bartender said as she put the scotch in front of Dennie.

"I'm having a rough morning," Dennie said. "People are thwarting me."

The redhead grinned at her. "Welcome to my world. And it's afternoon now, so maybe things will pick up."

"They can't get much worse." Dennie picked up her scotch. "Thanks. I needed this."

"My pleasure," the bartender said.

Dennie sipped her scotch, and the bartender drifted away as she contemplated her problem. Okay, she'd been shot down. She wasn't out yet. She could still get the interview somehow. In spite of Meredith's resistance and Trella's obtuseness and that manager's rabbitlike terror—

She closed her eyes as she felt every muscle she had tense with frustration. Be calm. Tension never got anybody anywhere. Tension was nonproductive. Tension was bad.

Calm was good. Calm. Cool. Sophisticated. If she was calm, she'd think of a solution. If she was calm, she could be charming again. She composed herself, opened her eyes, and looked at herself in the mirror over the bar. Exactly. She looked like an adult. She practiced a charming adult smile in the mirror.

"That is *some* smile."

Dennie whipped her head around. Standing beside her was the I've-got-plenty-of-money doofus from the lobby, all blank brown eyes and awshucks grin and dumb good looks. He looked a lot like the first guy she'd bumped into at the door, but bigger. Broader. In fact, if he hadn't had such a blank look on his face, he'd have been really attractive. He must have inherited his pile. He couldn't possibly have had the brains to make it himself. Not that it mattered. She had other things to concentrate on. "Go away."

"Aw, now, really." He slid onto the bar seat next to her and smiled at her like Walter when she picked up the treat can. Gee, gosh, ma'am. "I bet that smile gets you just about anything you want. Like dinner. It sure would get you dinner with me tonight."

The bartender had drifted back. Dennie caught her grinning and fought the urge to grin

back. "No, thank you. As I mentioned to you earlier, you have nothing I want. I would like to be
alone now, please." Dennie tried to turn her back
on him.

"Pretty lady like you, alone? Aw, c'mon." He
ducked his head in front of her, goofily confident.

Dennie reassessed her position on tension as
she clenched her teeth. "No, never, not in this lifetime, absolutely not," she said, enunciating each
word clearly, and the bartender bit her lip.

His eyes widened slightly, and he drew back.
"Gee, usually that smile bit is a great line for me."
He blinked at her. "But, hey, I'm adaptable. Okay.
Your smile is really bad."

Dennie swung around on her stool to walk
away from him before she killed him.

"And you're ugly too."

Dennie froze, and the bartender blinked.

"How am I doing?" the doofus asked, his
puppy smile still in place. "Better?"

Dennie shook her head, dumbstruck by his
cheerfulness. "I'm ugly?"

He nodded, his head bobbing like a fishing
float. "You probably walk funny too. That's why I

asked you to dinner. At least you'd be sitting down."

Dennie folded her arms. "My smile is bad, I'm ugly, and I walk funny."

He nodded again. "That's about it. So how about dinner?"

This guy made Walter look like Cary Grant. "As I said, not in this lifetime," Dennie said, and turned to walk out the door.

"Gee, and my aunt Trella seemed to like you so much."

Dennie swung back around to him. "Trella is your aunt?"

"Well, not really." He leaned back on the bar, looking dumb as dirt. "She's a friend of my aunt Victoria's."

"Victoria," Dennie said.

"Yep."

"Victoria's your aunt." Dennie came back to the bar and sat down, thinking fast. Not even Janice Meredith could have her arrested for talking to Victoria while she dated her nephew. She looked at him again, and he smiled, all teeth. Dear God.

Pretend he's Walter, she told herself. All she

had to do was be sweet to this twit, meet his aunt, be nice to the aunt, and she'd be in. She could do it. He wasn't bad looking or lecherous or evil, he was just dumb as a rock, which in this case was a plus. Maybe this was Fate apologizing. Dennie smiled at the twit. "I'd love to have dinner with you."

"Because of my aunt?" He looked confused. "Gee, I don't know."

Great, now he was playing hard to get. "Okay, then," Dennie said. "You're ugly."

His eyes locked on hers, and he grinned suddenly, and she was stunned. Humor leaped in his eyes, and a quick, sharp intelligence that disappeared as quickly as it came, replaced his blank childlike stare. *Hello,* she thought. *What's this?*

He aimed his Walter grin at her. "Well, if you're going to sweet-talk me, I'll consider it." He held out his hand. "I'm Alec Prentice."

She took it. "Dennie Banks." She looked in his eyes and saw nothing but blank affability. *You're up to something, sonny,* she thought, but all she said was, "I'll meet you here at seven, Alec Prentice."

"All right, Dennie Banks." Alec ducked his head again, doofus style. "You want dinner in the restaurant or in my room?"

"The restaurant," Dennie said. "You're not that ugly."

She dropped his hand and walked out of the bar, knowing he was watching.

For this, she'd left Walter. *You'd better be worth it, Alec Prentice,* she thought. *You'd better come across with everything I need.*

Then she went upstairs and changed into something Walter wouldn't have approved of.

"She's in it with him," Alec told Harry on the phone fifteen minutes later, trying not to gloat that he'd been right again and feeling vaguely depressed that he was.

"You found out already?"

"I tried to pick her up but it was no go until I mentioned my aunt, whom she's already been checking out. Once she heard about Aunt Vic, she couldn't wait to date me. She's working for Bond."

"Well, stay with her," Harry said. "I'll be there in a couple of hours. You sure your aunt will play along?"

"My aunt will play anything." Alec dismissed Victoria to think about Dennie Banks again. "You know, I really am disappointed in this Banks woman. Up close, she looks like a class act."

"You're getting too damn old to be that dumb," Harry said.

"Thank you, Harry," Alec said. "I needed that. Now tell me I'm ugly."

"You're ugly," Harry said. "Watch her."

Brian Bond studied his reflection in the mirror and nodded. He still had it, Sherée's desertion notwithstanding. The looks, the charm, the shy, boyish killer smile. They all said, "Trust me on this," and people did. Certainly no woman could resist once he set his sights on her.

And his sights were on the brunette. He'd seen her again, coming out of the bar that afternoon. A drinker. That was good. It'd make her easy to find. She'd be back in the bar again, he'd pour a few drinks down her, and pow. Another Bond triumph.

He smiled at his reflection and headed for the elevator to sell real estate and fake honesty before he sold the brunette on a night in his room.

When the brass elevator doors opened at the nineteenth floor, Alec stood face-to-face with a white-haired woman dressed in navy silk and gold braid. She beamed at him as she stepped in. "Darling!"

"Good. I was coming to talk to you." Alec leaned over and kissed her cheek, smiling because she was so cute and he was so glad to see her. "Nice getup, Aunt Vic. Planning on invading something?"

She laughed and saluted him as the elevator doors closed. "The military look is very stylish now. God knows why. Probably nostalgia for the Reagan years. But it's also wonderfully flattering. It's amazing how distracting gold braid can be." She frowned at the red velvet–covered elevator walls. "And it's not easy to stand out in this place. Who was their decorator, that Biddle Barrows woman?"

"I like it," Alec said.

"With your libido, you would," Victoria said. "What did you do all afternoon? Seduce the natives?"

"Waited for you, of course," Alec lied.

"Right." Victoria narrowed her eyes. "I left a message for you to meet me in the Ivy Room for lunch, but you didn't. What are you up to? Are you doing something for that secret agency of yours?"

"Shhhh," Alec said to the empty elevator.

"And you're awfully dressed up since you didn't know you'd run into me." His aunt looked at him in disgust. "You've picked up a blonde and asked her out to dinner, haven't you?"

"A brunette. Listen, I need—"

The elevator doors opened, and Victoria sailed out. "Don't worry," she said tartly. "I won't cramp your style."

Alec followed her with exasperated affection. "You never do. Most of the time I cramp yours."

Victoria sniffed. "Nobody cramps my style."

Alec caught up with her. "That's why I worry. You're running around with my last name, diving into fountains. Why didn't you keep your married name?"

"Why should I? I didn't keep my husband."

Alec tried to look stern. "It's time you settled down."

"Me?" Victoria snorted. "What about you?"

"Why should I settle down? I'm having a great time."

"That's your problem. You always have a great time." Victoria surveyed him critically. "You need some trauma in your life."

"Hey," Alec said. "I thought you loved me."

"I do," Victoria said over her shoulder as she headed for the restaurant. "But I worry about you. Things come too easily for you. Women, work, it all just falls into your lap."

"I work very hard at what I do. Which reminds me—"

Victoria turned in the middle of the lobby and nailed him with her eyes. "Have you ever failed? At anything?"

"Of course, I haven't failed." Alec was outraged. "I just told you—"

"If you haven't failed, you're not trying hard enough."

Alec glared at her. "Who told you this garbage?"

"A friend of mine. Janice Meredith."

"Meredith." Alec frowned. "The feminist whatsit. Marriage expert, right?"

"Yes." Victoria caught his sleeve and dragged him over to the row of gilt chairs he'd seen Dennie Banks use to con Trella that afternoon. "Sit down," she said and pushed him onto a chair as she sat down beside him. "Janice is going through a terrible time right now—I can't tell you why—but she's fine. And do you know why?"

Alec tried to be patient. "No, why?"

Victoria smacked his shoulder. "Pay attention and stop patronizing me. This is important. Janice says it's better to have taken a chance and tried, than never to have tried at all. If you haven't failed, you're only doing the easy things. A failure now and then tells you you're stretching yourself."

"So you want me to stretch myself and fail." Alec patted his aunt's hand. "No, thanks. Listen, I need you—"

"How long did it take you to get this woman to agree to dinner?"

"What?"

"This blonde you're having dinner with."

"Brunette."

"How long from the time you met her to the time she said yes?"

"About five minutes."

Victoria shook her head. "See, you're going for the easy victory."

"That's a terrible thing to say about a woman you've never met." Alec grinned at her. "And I hope to hell you're right."

"You know if you weren't so charming, you'd be a rat," Victoria said. "I'll be very relieved when you settle down."

"Is this lecture over yet?"

"Yes. Although you probably need a longer one."

"You have no idea what I need," Alec said. "For all you know, I'm vulnerable and lonely."

"Ha."

"Fine. Be that way. Now pay attention. I need a favor."

Victoria smiled at him fondly. "Anything, darling."

Alec smiled back in spite of himself. "Did I mention I've missed you?"

"Oh, I've missed you, too, darling." Victoria patted his knee. "That's why I sent you the invitation. I'm going to fix your life this weekend."

"No, you're not," Alec said. "Drop that idea entirely and listen. I need you to buy some real estate from a con man. And then I will arrest him."

"A con man?" Victoria frowned. "I thought you were on vacation."

"I am," Alec said. "This is a freebie. Pure luck. My boss is flying in late tonight to talk to both of us. Can we meet you at eleven in your room?"

"Of course," Victoria said. "It sounds like fun."

"Well, it's not." Alec scowled at her. "This is serious work."

"This is what you do for a living?"

"Yes."

She shrugged. "Then how serious can it be?"

Alec stood. "On that note, I will leave you for my date. Would you like to join us for dinner?" he added politely, knowing Victoria would never do anything that dumb.

"I'd love to," she said, standing, too, and Alec started. "But I have a date of my own." Alec glared at her, and Victoria grinned back unfazed. "That'll teach you to make invitations you don't mean." Her eyes focused over Alec's left shoulder, and when he turned to see, she waved to a distinguished graying man who was smiling at her. "There's my date. I'm hoping he's not going to be the stuffed shirt I'm pretty sure he's going to be."

"Wait." Alec caught her arm as she moved past him. "I need—"

Victoria waved her hand at him. "Go amuse your blonde. And call me when your boss gets in."

"Brunette," Alec said in exasperation, but he let her go and watched her move toward the stuffed shirt who beamed his appreciation. "Bad choice, Aunt Vic," he said to himself, and then stopped. The stuffed shirt looked like prime Bond material. Maybe he should encourage Victoria to cultivate a taste for the overstuffed this weekend.

Victoria and her date went into the restaurant, and Alec checked his watch and headed for the bar. Enough about Victoria's dating problems; he was late to meet a beautiful crook.

❧

Chapter 3

Dennie walked into the bar at seven and ordered a daiquiri. The bartender slid the frosted glass in front of her, and she opened her purse.

"Let me get that," someone beside her said, and she turned to see the *g*-dropping farm boy from the hotel door that afternoon, smiling at her shyly.

"Brian Bondman." He offered her his hand. "We ran into each other this morning."

He ducked his head and smiled again, and Dennie wondered why she'd suddenly begun attracting men with weak necks. All this ducking and peering up at her. There was enough aw shucks in this hotel to gag a maggot. Still, he was being nice, so Dennie shook his hand with tepid enthusiasm, but when he put some bills on the bar, she slid them back to him.

"I prefer to pay for my own drink, thank you."

"Ah, you're independent." He shook his head at her apologetically. "Well, then . . ." He leaned closer, and she could see the deep blue of his eyes. He was probably doing that because he thought women loved deep blue eyes. He should have tried it on another woman. Dennie could spot colored contacts a mile away. He smiled at her. "How about letting me pay for dinner?"

Someone tapped on Bondman's shoulder, and Dennie turned to see her date for the evening. *John-Boy meets Opie,* she thought. *Get me out of here.*

"That's not a bad line, but I used it earlier," Alec told him. "Sorry."

Bondman stopped smiling for an instant, and Dennie thought there might be a fight. Clash of the Nerds. She opened her mouth to head them off, but then Alec smiled at Bondman like a half-wit, and Bondman smiled back, much the same smile, and said, "No problem. Maybe my timing will get better later."

"Oh, it's bound to get better," Alec said, clapping Bondman on the back. "No hard feelings, right?" He looked past Bondman and smiled at Dennie. "You look super," he told her. "Let's go have dinner so I can show you off."

Dennie looked at them both. It was a good time to be giving up men if this was what the planet had to offer. If it wasn't for needing Alec's aunt to convince Janice Meredith—

Alec looked her up and down. "Great dress," he said. "Gosh."

It was going to be a long evening. She held out her hand. "Lead on, Macduff."

"Actually, that's 'lay on.'" Alec took her hand and helped her off the bar stool. "It's what Macbeth said right before he lost his head."

"Well, don't count on it happening again." Dennie pulled him toward the door and away from Brian Bondman. "I'm hungry, but I'm not about to lose my head."

* * *

Bond watched them go. The guy in the suit had to be one of those college professors. Talking like a hayseed and quoting *Macbeth*. Fine. He'd take him for every cent he had. And then he'd take the woman away from him too. He turned back to the bar and brooded on his plans for revenge and profit while he drank Dennie's daiquiri.

"So where did you learn *Macbeth*?" Dennie asked Alec when they'd been seated in the restaurant on gilt chairs, separated from each other by three quarters of a yard of virgin linen and an ornate brass candleholder covered with brass ivy. "Classic comics?"

"My aunt Vic is a British lit professor." Alec moved the candleholder to one side. He absent-mindedly turned it upside down to look at the bottom of the holder, and as Dennie said, "No!" the candle fell out and rolled to the edge of the table, still burning. He lunged to get it and knocked over his water glass as Dennie caught the candle. "Sorry," he said sheepishly.

Dennie took the holder from him and replaced

the candle before she set it to one side. She narrowed her eyes at him, suddenly suspicious. That whole move had seemed, well, false somehow. "Your aunt," she prompted him as she mopped up the water with her napkin.

"Uh, right. My aunt." Alec furrowed his brow as he concentrated. "She made my brother and me each pick a play from Shakespeare one summer in exchange for hauling us to a cottage on Lake Michigan. My brother, the history nut, grabbed *Henry V*. I asked her if there was anything with a lot of killing and—"

"She gave you *Macbeth*."

"Actually she gave me a choice between *Hamlet* and *Macbeth*."

Dennie held up her hand. "Don't tell me. Let me guess. You counted the pages."

"Yep." Alec grinned. "My aunt didn't raise no dummies."

Dennie began to revise her opinion of him. He was good-looking if you liked dumb grins and boyish enthusiasm. And there was something else there, something about that flash she'd seen in his eyes in the bar. And the whole bit with the candle wasn't right. He moved with too much grace to be that clumsy. He was up to something, and he definitely would bear watching. But the most important thing was that he was talking about his aunt without any prompting from her. She felt very warm toward him for that, so she smiled at him. "So did it work? Did you like *Macbeth*?"

"Yep," Alec said. "It was great. In fact, my aunt and I are still arguing about the third murderer. Nobody knows who it was."

"Sure they do." Dennie sipped her water. "It was Macduff."

Alec shook his head. "It couldn't be. Macduff was one of the good guys. Why would he kill Banquo?"

"He didn't," Dennie said patiently. "He put out the light so Banquo's son could escape. It's obvious."

"What is obvious is that it was Lady Macbeth," Alec said. "End of question."

Dennie shook her head in disgust. "Are you out of your mind? It couldn't have been Lady Macbeth. She was back at the castle throwing a party. Did you actually read this play?" She glared at him, so caught up in the conversation that she forgot to be charming, and he gaped at her.

Alec took a minute to answer her because she was having an unexpected effect on him. Nothing he couldn't handle, but still. . . . She had lightning in her eyes, and an incredibly lush mouth, and she was bright, very bright. It was hard to believe that she was working with Bond. If he hadn't seen them together twice now . . . Alec tried to concentrate on the argument to lull her into a false sense of security, but her eyes kept distracting him. "How come you know *Macbeth* so well?"

Dennie narrowed her eyes. "I did my senior honors thesis on it. Now stop changing the subject. How could Lady Macbeth possibly be the third murderer?"

Alec tried to look dumber than usual. "She could have snuck out before the party. There was time."

"How?" Dennie shook her head at him, clearly amazed. "She was Queen of Scotland, and it was a state banquet. It's not like they were having the

Macduffs over for hot dogs. She could not have *snuck out* and stabbed Banquo. Where is your mind?"

"Hey." Alec was stung by her criticism even while he knew he was being unreasonable. Of course, she thought he was dumb. He was acting dumb. Still . . . "Lady Macbeth masterminded the whole thing."

"She did not. She didn't even know he was doing it. It's in the play that he doesn't tell her until afterward."

"Ha," Alec said. "She pretended not to know."

Dennie studied him. "Is it indicative of some deep-seated hostility toward women that you are willing to frame her for a crime she didn't commit? Or are you really this dumb?"

"Dumb?" Alec bristled again. "Hell, she'd already killed Duncan."

"No, she didn't. Macbeth killed Duncan."

"Yeah, but he wouldn't have if she hadn't egged him on. That woman was a bitch."

Dennie leaned back and folded her arms. "That's what all insecure men call powerful women."

Alec leaned back and folded his arms. "Do not tell me you are a feminist."

"Of course I'm a feminist, you moron. What did you think I was?"

"I was hoping you were a bimbo. Unfortunately, I was wrong."

Dennie's laugh startled him. "I like you." She leaned forward and picked up a breadstick. "Your grasp of *Macbeth* is pathetic, but you may have other possibilities. And you're not nearly as dumb as you're pretending to be. What is all that about anyway?" She crunched into the stick, her even white teeth neatly severing the bread.

"All what?" Alec asked, caught flat-footed, and then the waiter brought the menus.

"Would you like to see the wine list, sir?"

"Sure." Alec took the wine list from him with gratitude. He looked across the top of the folder at Dennie. "Any preferences?"

"Nope," Dennie said. "Stun me with your expertise."

Alec snapped the wine list back to the waiter. "Something in a red."

"I'm stunned," Dennie said.

The waiter looked pained. "Very good, sir."

"Do you know that blond guy at the bar very well?" Alec asked her when the waiter was gone.

"Not at all." Dennie studied her menu. "What's good to eat here?"

"I hear everything is good here." Alec stared at her while she considered the menu. She was too smart to be working for Bond. Maybe he was working for her. That was a depressing thought. It was going to take a lot of work to get the truth out of her. He might even have to have sex with her to get it. That was not a depressing thought.

The waiter came back with the wine.

Alec touched his glass to hers and looked deep into her eyes, smiling his best vulnerable-puppy smile. "To the start of something wonderful."

"Probably not," Dennie said, and drank.

Alec stopped his glass halfway to his mouth. "Probably not?"

Dennie nodded. "I'm giving up guys like you to concentrate on my career. That's why I need to meet your aunt. I should probably have told you that earlier. Should we go dutch on dinner?"

Alec looked confused. It was a look he was

quite good at faking, but talking with Dennie made it even easier than usual. "Uh, no, I have plenty of money. What do you mean, guys like me?"

Dennie sipped her wine. "You know. Sophisticated. Charming. Good with wine lists. What is it that you do that gets you plenty of money?"

"Investments." That should interest her. Alec frowned at her, knowing he should concentrate on the investments part but wanting to pursue other things. "So why are you giving me up if I'm all of that?"

"Because right now I'm at a turning point in my career. I have to give it everything I've got." Dennie dismissed him with her hand. "I can't fritter away my time on dinner and sex with guys like you. What kind of investments?"

"Land." Alec meant to go on waxing eloquent about his big investment habits, but instead he said, "And you couldn't have had this realization later in the week? My timing has reached an all-time low."

"I'd feel bad about this, but obviously you're not going to suffer." Dennie surveyed him critically.

"You're one of those boyishly good-looking types. You probably never suffer. Actually, a little suffering might do you good."

Alec scowled at her. "Did my aunt put you up to this?"

Dennie looked interested. "No. Let's talk about your aunt. She's out to get you? Why?"

The waiter interrupted them.

"Separate checks, please," Dennie said.

"Ignore her," Alec said. "She's having an independent fit. With any luck, it will go away."

"No chance," Dennie said. "But if it bothers you that much, I'll let you pay for dinner."

"Would you care to order?" the waiter asked, confused but determined.

Dennie studied the menu. "You're in trouble. I'm starving."

Alec tried to recapture his doofus persona. "Good. I love a woman who eats hearty."

"Well, then . . ." She smiled up at the waiter. "Prime rib, very rare. Asparagus. Cheddar cheese baked potato. Ranch dressing on the salad."

"Same for me," Alec said, snapping his menu

closed, and the waiter rolled his eyes and left. "Now about sex—"

"Tell me about your aunt." Dennie bit into her breadstick again, and he watched her mouth move and lost his place in the conversation. "Why does she hate you?"

"My aunt?" Alec looked away from her mouth so he could think. "She doesn't hate me. She adores me. She just thinks I need more trauma in my life."

Dennie stopped chewing. "Trauma?"

Alec picked up a breadstick of his own. "Things come easy for me. Always have." He scowled at her. "Until you. She thinks it would be good if I failed for once."

"She's right," Dennie said. "She's absolutely right. That's why I'm getting serious about my career."

"So I can have trauma?"

"No. So *I* can. I'm like you. Everything's always been easy for me. But I think that's because I haven't tried anything tough, you know? And then I overheard Janice Meredith in the restaurant this afternoon. She said that if you're not failing every now and then, you're not trying hard enough. And I've never failed."

Alec snapped his breadstick in half. "I have a score to settle with Janice Meredith."

Dennie leaned forward. "Do you know Janice Meredith?"

Alec looked down the neck of her dress. She was wearing a purple lace bra, and she was rounder than he'd imagined. "Don't move for a minute, will you?"

Dennie tapped him on the nose with her breadstick. "Pay attention. Do . . . you . . . know . . . Janice . . . Meredith?"

"No," Alec said, enjoying the view. "But my aunt does. You know, Thursday is a notoriously bad day for making decisions. Maybe you ought to reconsider—"

"Sleeping with a man I just met whose main occupation seems to be staring at my breasts? No." Dennie leaned back. "You're cute, Alec, but my Yorkie, Walter, is deeper than you are. My next relationship, which is going to be several years in the future when my career is well-established, is also going to be my last, and it's going to be deep. Tell me about your aunt."

"I'm deep," Alec said, and then grinned. "Okay, I may be no match for Walter, but I have depths. And if you were deep, you wouldn't be wearing that dress or that underwear. Purple lace? No."

Dennie looked down. "You're right. This calls for a whole new wardrobe."

"No, it doesn't," Alec began, but their salads arrived, and Dennie attacked hers. She had a good, healthy appetite, he noticed. That usually boded well for other things. If she hadn't decided to give up other things. Maybe he could convince her not to give them up yet, all in the line of duty, of course. He tried to imagine explaining to Harry how seducing Dennie fell in the line of duty.

The hell with Harry.

Unfortunately she wanted deep, and he'd been projecting dumb. And if he was going to be honest, deep was not in his repertoire anyway. Smart, yes; brave, yes; fast-thinking, yes; honest, yes. Deep, no. But he might be able to fake it.

"Tell me about your career," Alec said.

"Why?" Dennie looked at him suspiciously from behind a forkful of dripping greens.

"I want to know why you're giving up the best sex you would have ever had for some dumb job."

"Okay, that sounds more like you," Dennie said, and ate her salad.

"More like me?"

"For a minute there, I thought you were trying to be sensitive," Dennie said after she'd swallowed. "With you, that could only mean one thing."

Alec tried to look blank and insulted at the same time. "Thank you."

Dennie shrugged. "Don't get annoyed. I just know your kind. You sure you don't want me to pay for dinner?"

"Positive." Alec fought back his annoyance. "So what's this career?"

Dennie looked wary suddenly. "You wouldn't be interested. The important thing is, your aunt can help me. Please notice that I'm being very upfront here. I want you to introduce me to your aunt and tell her I'm a wonderful person."

"Why?" Alec said warily.

"Because I want to talk to her. All I need is for you to tell her that I'm clean, brave, and reverent, and convince her to talk to me. I'll do the rest."

Alec sat back. "What do you want from her?"

Dennie shook her head. "That's confidential. I'd tell you, but it's not my secret."

She blotted some salad dressing from her lips, and Alec repressed his instincts. They were great lips, but it looked more and more as though he wouldn't be getting access to them because he'd be arresting her, so he tried to ignore them and concentrate on what she was saying.

"So will you do it?" she asked.

"What?" Alec said.

Dennie closed her eyes in pain. "Introduce me to your aunt, dummy. Why are you acting like this?"

"Like what?" Alec said.

"Like you're a moron," Dennie said. "Is this some kind of weird pickup thing you do that attracts women? Because I've got to tell you, I like you smart and sassy a lot better."

"Sassy?" Alec said. "Me?"

"Forget it," Dennie said. "Concentrate on your aunt. When can I meet her?"

"You know, I wasn't expecting you to be this pushy," Alec said. "You're not what I was expecting at all."

"What were you expecting?"

"Well, I was hoping for easy."

Dennie nodded. "That's right. You thought I was a bimbo. We already did this."

Alec looked hopeful. "You walk like a bimbo."

"I do not." Dennie leaned back in her chair and looked at him with critical eyes. "But you do."

"I do not."

"Yeah, you do. All shoulders. Big man in town. You come on like a flashlight. You should have 'Eveready' printed on your forehead."

Alec raised his eyebrows. "And that sway you left the bar with today was professional? Jaws were dropping all around you."

"Look, I have hips. They move."

"They certainly do. And I wouldn't dream of criticizing them if you hadn't made fun of my shoulders."

"I wasn't making fun." Dennie batted her eyes

at him. "They're wonderful shoulders. Shoulders to die for. Shoulders that beg to be wept on. Shoulders—"

"Thank you, that will do," Alec said. "I may make you pay for dinner after all."

"Forget it." Dennie eyed the steaming platter that the waiter put in front of her. "Fighting with you has given me an appetite. I want dessert too." She looked up sharply as Alec opened his mouth. "Do not say anything juvenile about what you can give me for dessert."

"Juvenile?" Alec looked up at the waiter. "Is there anything about me that strikes you as juvenile?"

"No, sir," the waiter said.

"Now ask me," Dennie said.

"Don't," Alec said.

"So, about your aunt," Dennie began again.

Alec closed his eyes. This was what he wanted, Dennie making a move on Victoria. It would have been really bad if she'd made a move on him instead. They'd never nail her for fraud if all she did was seduce him. He opened his eyes. "Are you sure you're giving up sex?"

"Positive," Dennie said. "When can I meet your aunt?"

Across the room, Victoria was having her own trauma.

"Well, this is certainly pleasant," Donald Compton said, beaming at her across the snowy linen of the tablecloth.

Pleasant, Victoria thought. *I'm sixty-two years old. Screw pleasant. I want exciting.*

Donald consulted with the waiter on the wine list. He looked wonderful consulting with the waiter. Handsome, distinguished, debonair. They made a nice couple, Donald and the waiter. Maybe she should leave them alone. After all, Donald and the waiter had so much more in common than Donald and she did.

Donald and she. Ugly little phrase. She speculated aimlessly about a future with Donald. Donald and she would buy property on the Cape; the exclusive section, of course. Donald and she would vacation in Belize; he'd want someplace not spoiled by the tourist trade. Donald and she would drive a Mercedes; it would be the only car that didn't clash with his Rolex.

Donald and she, Victoria decided, were doomed as a couple. He hadn't even cracked the wine, and already she was making fun of him.

Donald turned back to her and toasted her with his glass. It was full. He and the waiter must have achieved climax while she was daydreaming.

"To you," he said. "You look elegant."

Elegant. Wonderful. "You too." She raised her glass to him and then looked past him and saw Alec. He was leaning toward a brunette, but all Victoria could see of the woman was the back of a head full of glossy dark curls. Alec smiled, and Victoria thought, *How can she resist him? He has the family charm.*

"Victoria?"

"Hmmm?" Victoria looked at her glass, still in midair. "Oh, yes. To both of us. Elegant. Absolutely." She drank her wine and remembered what Janice had said about risking. The only thing she was risking by being with Donald Compton was death from boredom.

Donald began to tell her about a wonderful

real estate investment a man he'd met in the bar that afternoon had told him about. Victoria began to tune him out and then remembered what Alec had said.

"What's this man's name?" she asked. "Tell me all about him."

"This was wonderful," Dennie said, blotting her mouth again after they'd cruised through their entrées. "Thank you for not making small talk during dinner. It would have ruined everything."

Alec winced. "You know, you're not good for my ego."

Dennie looked apologetic. "That's not what I meant. I meant—"

"I know what you meant." He grinned at her. "I feel the same way. Why mess up great food by trying to think about something else?"

"Exactly." Dennie smiled at him, and his head reeled for a minute.

Concentrate, he told himself. *She's a crook.* "About my aunt." He threw Victoria out like a lifeline.

"I need to talk to her," Dennie said. "If she'll help me, I could make it big. Out of the minor leagues, into the majors."

"The majors?"

"New York."

"You want to work in New York?" Alec shook his head. "Mistake. Come to Chicago. Much nicer city."

"What's in Chicago?"

"Me," Alec said, and then wondered why he'd said it. It was pretty stupid telling a woman to move to a major city so he could have dinner with her occasionally, especially since he was planning on arresting her. Of course, stupid was the personality he was trying to project, but still. It was humiliating being stupid in front of Dennie Banks.

"You think I should move to Chicago because you're there? After one dinner?" Dennie shook her head. "There's a dim bulb in your flashlight."

Alec opened his mouth to retort and then closed it. He'd asked for that one.

"So when can I meet your aunt?" Dennie asked.

"Have lunch with me tomorrow," Alec said. "I

cannot guarantee my aunt will be there, but I'll try. How about one? I have a late meeting tonight."

Dennie beamed at him. "Terrific." She sipped the last of her wine and said, "What kind of meeting do you have?"

"Hey," Alec said. "You want the intimate details of my life, you have to get intimate."

Dennie frowned at him in disbelief. "I have to sleep with you to find out about your meetings?"

He gazed at her hopefully. "Would that do it?"

"No," Dennie said. "You are achieving a new low in superficial here."

"My aunt's going to like you," Alec said.

"I'm devastated at having to leave you, Victoria," Donald said as he pressed her hand at her hotel room door. "If only I hadn't made plans to speak with this Bondman fellow about the investment."

"Perfectly all right," Victoria said, trying to disengage her hand.

"It really is a wonderful investment. Florida

beach-front property. Perhaps you'd like to join us?"

"Not tonight, Donald." Victoria smiled up at him as she shoved her card in the door and opened it. "But perhaps tomorrow. For dinner. Do you think you could arrange it?"

"Delighted to!" Donald said. "And who knows? Maybe we could invest in something together. Like our futures?" He raised an arched eyebrow at her.

"Who knows?" Victoria sidled inside her door. "Until then."

"Until then." Donald leaned forward to kiss her, and she shut the door in his face. Then she leaned against it, relieved to be alone.

The things she did for her nephew. And now she had to play hostess to Alec's grumpy old boss.

Still, he had to be better than Donald.

Anybody was better than Donald.

Dennie continued to battle with Alec during the elevator ride to her room, cheerfully insulting him at regular intervals because he seemed to enjoy it.

He had either no ego at all or the healthiest ego on the planet. She studied him when they stopped in the dim light of the hallway outside her room. He stood before her, carelessly relaxed and lazily confident.

He definitely had an ego.

He was also definitely a mystery. He was a lot smarter than he looked and a lot more dangerous. She was positive that his aw-shucks innocence was a cover-up for a devious, twisted mind. Too bad her career was on the line. Exploring Alec could have been educational, and since he wasn't the easy kind of guy she'd dated before, Patience would have been pleased too. "Look what I found in a hotel bar," she could say, towing Alec behind her like show-and-tell at school. "Ignore the dumb act. This one is complicated."

"Lunch at one," Alec said, and she turned her face up to him, startled into remembering him.

"One," she started to say, but he kissed her while she was puckering her mouth to say the word. He stepped on her toe, and bumped her nose with his, and then missed her mouth at first, but when he found it, clumsily, he tasted so good that she leaned into him slightly, touching his lips with her tongue.

And then suddenly he changed; his kiss stopped bumbling and became solid and deep, and he slid his arms around her and pulled her close. He felt so good against her that she wound her arms around his neck and pressed herself to him. Heat washed over her, and evidently over him, too, because by the time she broke the kiss, he had her plastered up against the wall, his thigh between hers, his tongue licking her mouth while she gasped for breath.

And when he lifted his face from hers, he looked as surprised as she was.

"Listen, I could learn to be deep," he told her, and she said, "Shut up and kiss me again," and he did, teasing her mouth with his tongue until she opened to him, and they both sagged boneless against the wall. His hand found her breast and made her shiver and then moved up to the draped neck of her dress and inside it, and when she felt the shock of his fingers on her skin, she remembered where she was and all her plans and how he wasn't part of them no matter how damn good his hand felt inside her dress.

She caught his wrist. "Wait a minute. I forgot. I don't have time for this. I'm sorry. I just forgot."

Alec moved his hand to her waist. "Give me another chance. I'll make you forget again. I'll make you forget your name." He bent to kiss her again, and she ducked away.

"No. Thank you, but no. Good-bye. Lovely evening. Can't wait to meet your aunt." Dennie turned while she babbled and jammed her key card in the door, and before he could say anything else, she'd slipped inside and closed the door in his face.

Whoa. She let her head fall back against the door. This boy was definitely nobody to mess with. At least not while she was in the middle of career building.

What a shame.

Harry called Alec's room when he got to the hotel at ten-forty-five.

"What've you got?" he asked when Alec picked up the phone.

"Don't you ever start with 'Hello'?"

"No," Harry said. "What've you got?"

"I've got Dennie Banks doing everything in her power to meet my aunt." Alec thought about Dennie's kiss. "And Harry, she's got a lot of power. If she tries to seduce me into a life of crime, I'm going for it."

Harry snorted. "You should be so lucky. What else?"

"Aunt Victoria's in. We're meeting in her room as soon as I call her."

Harry scowled. "I hate the Aunt Victoria part."

"Harry, you haven't met her yet."

"I don't like the idea of sending in a little old lady to meet Bond."

Alec tried not to laugh. "Aunt Vic is no little old lady. Hell, she's only a couple years older than you are."

"I don't care," Harry said. "I don't like it."

"Too bad. I'll call her now. Room 1914 in ten minutes," Alec said. "Don't be late."

* * *

Harry knocked on the door to room 1914, steeling himself to be nice to the little old lady. He was so prepared that he was looking down with the closest thing he had to a reassuring smile on his face when she opened the door.

The problem was that Victoria was only two inches shorter than he was so that instead of looking down into a kindly little-old-lady face, he found himself looking down into the V neck of her navy silk dress.

She didn't look like a little old lady.

Victoria followed his gaze down. "I lift weights. I may not be defeating gravity, but I'm giving it a run for its money."

"What?" Harry said.

"You must be Harry Chase. Alec told me about you. I'm Victoria Prentice." Victoria held out a perfectly manicured hand, and Harry took it, his stunned gaze traveling from her cleavage to her face. She had Alec's eyes—bright brown eyes— and his sharp, mobile mouth, but she was all female where Alec was male. Her hair was styled short and framed her face in soft white curls, and she was wearing small gold earrings. Expensive gold earrings. She should have looked attractive, elegant, and remote, but there was a glint in her eye and a quirk to her lips that gave her away.

This is a dangerous woman, Harry thought, acting on the instincts that had kept him alive and single for fifty-eight years. *This is a woman who has been places and done things and who has ideas of her own.*

Get me out of here.

He turned to go, but Alec came up behind him and slapped him on the back. "Good to see you, Harry," he said, and crowded him into Victoria's room, and then it was too late to run.

Victoria stepped back to let them in. She had thoroughly enjoyed Harry's reaction, but now she was taken aback to notice how much he resembled Alec. It wasn't the physical details so much. Alec's brown hair was always neatly combed while Harry's iron-gray mop looked like it was permanently rumpled; Harry's jaw jutted more than

Alec's, and his shoulders were a little broader; Harry's eyes were black and snapping compared to Alec's warm brown gaze. No one would mistake them for relatives.

It was the way they stood, she decided. And moved. And looked around a room. Big men so confident, they couldn't imagine a situation they couldn't handle. That agency they both worked for must train them to be that way. No one could be born as sure of himself as these two were.

Alec pulled chairs out from the desk in the corner of the room, waving to them as he spoke. "Victoria, this is Harry Chase, my boss. Harry, this is my aunt, Victoria Prentice."

"We've done that already," Victoria said. "Should I call down to room service for coffee?"

"Hell, no," Harry growled. "This isn't a party."

"No, thank you, Aunt Vic," Alec said. "It's getting late, so I'll just give you the basics and let Harry fill in the rest, and then we can all get some sleep."

Victoria sat down and smiled sweetly at Harry because she knew it would disconcert him. Harry scowled at her.

Alec looked at both of them, confused. "Have you two met before?"

"Oh, no," Victoria said. "I'd have remembered Harry."

"Can we get on with this?" Harry said.

"Sure," Alec began but Harry overrode him, turning to Victoria as he spoke.

"There's a guy in this hotel going by the name of Brian Bondman who's made a career out of bilking college professors," he told her.

"What's his real name?" Victoria asked.

"Forget it," Harry said. "If you don't know it, you can't use it accidentally and screw everything up."

"Harry," Alec said. "Be nice."

Victoria tried to wither Harry with a glance, but he ignored her and went on. "We've almost had him a couple of times, but he's gotten away through sheer dumb luck."

"Dumb luck," Victoria sniffed. "Sounds like an excuse."

"Aunt Vic," Alec warned.

"Well, he's here now, and we're going to get him this time," Harry said. "And Alec's brainstorm is to use you to nail him." His tone of voice made it clear how he felt about that plan.

"We want you to make contact with him," Alec told her. "Be your usual charming self and talk about your money and your investments. You know, act rich."

"What if he checks me out?" Victoria said. "I'm not rich."

Harry looked at her gold earrings, silk blouse, and perfect hair, and snorted. Victoria ignored him.

"Harry, knock it off." Alec turned back to Victoria. "He won't, Aunt Vic. You're a professor and that's enough for him. He'll see your name in the conference program and figure he's home free."

"He can't be too bright if he's targeting college professors," Victoria said. "We're not known for being wealthy."

"Depends on your definition of 'wealthy,'" Harry said. "You're sure not poor."

Victoria ignored him some more. "Any ideas on how I meet this man?"

"There's a woman," Alec said. "Dennie Banks.

She'll introduce you to him. In fact, she can't wait. You're having lunch with her tomorrow."

Victoria rolled her eyes at him. "I can't, I'm having lunch with Janice. I should have known you'd find a woman. Is this your blonde?"

"Brunette," Alec said automatically. "And you have to ditch Janice for Dennie because Dennie is going to introduce you to her partner, and he's the one we want."

Victoria turned to Harry. "And after I'm introduced, then what?"

"Then we put a wire on you, and we've got him," Harry said. "That's the theory anyway."

"A wire?" Victoria looked nonplussed.

"Don't you ever watch TV cop shows?" Harry asked.

"No." Victoria put her chin in the air. "I'm an intellectual."

"You are not." Alec glared at both of them. "I don't know what's wrong with you two, but snap out of it. You've got work to do. Act like adults. This is no time to start a second childhood."

"A wire," Harry said with palpable patience,

"is a very small microphone and transmitter. What he says to you, we will hear and tape."

"Big deal." Victoria sniffed. "I don't see what's so tough about this."

Harry sighed. "That's what I'm afraid of."

"In fact, we don't even need your blonde, Alec, so I can still have lunch with Janice," Victoria went on. "I'm already having dinner with Mr. Bondman tomorrow evening. A friend is introducing us because of the wonderful real estate investment Mr. Bondman is offering." She batted her eyes at Harry. "And they pay you to do this. Really, it's so simple."

"You're what?" Alec said, startled.

"It was so simple," Victoria repeated. "You didn't need to seduce that woman after all."

"I didn't seduce her," Alec said.

"Not for lack of trying, I'm sure." Victoria gazed at him with pseudosympathy. "Did she turn you down? How marvelous for you. See, you're failing already. Do you feel any character growth?"

"Aunt Vic," Alec began, and Harry stood up and interrupted him.

"I'll call you tomorrow morning and set up a time for the wire," he told Victoria.

She shook her head. "Not tomorrow morning. My paper is tomorrow morning and so is Janice's. Tomorrow afternoon."

Harry gave up. "Fine. But do not go near Bond until I've got you wired."

"Bondman," Victoria said. "I gather Bond is his real name. How careless of you to let it slip."

"Aunt Vic," Alec said. "That's enough."

"Thank you," Harry said to him. "I was hoping somebody would say that."

"You have to work with Harry," Alec told his aunt. "And Harry is not a nice man. Do not antagonize him."

"He antagonized me first," Victoria said.

"Oh, that's mature," Alec said. "Listen, both of you. Try not to call each other names until after we've nailed Bond, okay?"

"All right," Victoria said. "I apologize, Harry."

Harry growled, and stomped out of the room.

Alec bent and kissed her cheek. "Harry's sorry too. Get some sleep. You're going to be trapping a major menace to society tomorrow."

"Would that be Harry?" Victoria asked sweetly.

"Good night, Aunt Vic," Alec said sternly, and left her.

Victoria started to laugh as soon as the door closed behind him. She'd been right. Harry was better than Donald.

A lot better.

Donald Compton met Brian Bond in the bar at eleven; by eleven-thirty, they were elbow-deep in a prospectus for an exclusive real estate development in the Keys. Bond felt his pulse kick up as he explained the deal and Donald nodded in agreement at every turn. The perfect mark, God bless him, and he was all Bond's.

"This is very hush-hush," Bond said. "But the great thing about this investment is that there's nobody else even interested in this property because of the environmental impact hassles. We're getting the land at rock-bottom prices."

"EPA, though, Brian. That's bad." Donald looked owlishly wise.

"Nah," Bond said. "We've got somebody in

Washington. The fix will be in by the end of the month. And the land values will shoot through the roof."

Donald brightened considerably, and Bond moved in for the kill. "Now here's what I'd recommend you invest . . ."

Eight miles away, Sherée got off the bus at the Riverbend bus terminal and stretched. A day of bus travel had not made her feel any better about her life. She'd find a cheap motel for the night, she decided, and then track Brian down the next day. She picked up her suitcase and headed for the neon motel sign she could see two blocks down.

It was a hassle that she'd forgotten the name of the hotel, she thought as she trudged along, but how many places could be having a literature conference? Tomorrow she'd start calling around. And then she'd find Brian.

And then they'd see what was going to happen, boy.

Then they'd see.

Chapter 4

Dennie left the room the next morning in the good gray suit that she wore only when she wanted to impress people with her seriousness. It did double duty in that it also impressed *her* with her seriousness. She slipped into the back of the lecture room, feeling very focused and mature, just as the previous speaker sat down, and Janice Meredith stood to present her paper.

It was an exploration of how the infidelity in Shakespeare might be handled by the modern scandal pulps, and Dennie almost wept with sympathy for her as she listened to her. No wonder the woman didn't want anyone to know about her divorce yet; she couldn't have chosen a more painful topic. And yet, even as she felt for her, Dennie made notes. There were too many parallels there to ignore. If she got the interview, she could help Janice present her case. If she got the interview, she could protect her while—

No, wait, not *if*. When. Dennie smoothed the skirt of her gray suit. *When* she got her interview, she'd use some of these same points to showcase Janice's strengths. It was going to be a great interview, a triumph for both Dennie and Janice.

Then the next presenter got up, and Dennie saw with some surprise that it was Victoria Prentice. She'd been so fixated on Janice that she'd forgotten Victoria was an academic too. Victoria's paper was a comparison of the Macbeths' marriage to television soap opera marriages, and Macbeth made Dennie think of Alec the night before. What was Victoria saying about the Macbeths? "Flawed people united by love, destroyed by ambition." Well, she and Alec were definitely flawed. She was ambitious, and she was pretty sure Alec was too. That dumb act was just that, an act; he was up to something with those land investments.

And the love? That was the disconcerting part. Because there was something about Alec . . . Dennie tried to isolate what it was about Alec, and then realized that for the first time she'd met a man she wouldn't grow tired of. She might want to strangle him in the future, but she wouldn't get bored. He would always be unpredictable and sexy and up to something. He was the first man she'd ever known who made more than one date together seem like an interesting idea.

Patience would have loved Alec.

Of course, all that was an excellent reason to avoid him once he'd introduced her to Victoria. She was not going to end up in Chicago, chasing Alec, when she could be moving anywhere, New York even, and chasing fame and a huge career. She'd made enough dumb decisions in her life already. Time for some smart ones.

No matter how tempting Alec was.

While Dennie thought about Alec, Victoria finished her paper, and the next presenter got up and began to speak about marriage customs in Shakespeare's era and in the nineties. Dennie slipped out of the room as quietly as she'd slipped in. If

Janice Meredith had sparked some interview ideas in the presentation today, there must be more in her other writings. A good interviewer couldn't be too well-prepared, and Riverbend U was only a couple of miles away.

Dennie headed for the university library.

Two hours later, she met Alec for lunch.

"Where's your aunt?" she asked, coming up behind him in the lobby. His shoulders were broad and his back was straight, and she had random, inappropriate thoughts about his body before he turned to her, startled, and she was pleasantly surprised to remember how much fun his face was to look at when he wasn't letting his mouth hang open.

"Who died?" Alec said, staring at her gray suit. "Gray? This isn't like you. Tell me there's red lace under that."

"Your aunt," Dennie said, full of drive after an excellent hour in the library stacks. She had the right questions now, and Janice Meredith was going to answer them. The interview of a lifetime. Dennie looked around for Victoria, her ticket to Janice, fame, and fortune. "Where is she?"

"She couldn't make it." Alec still stared at her suit in obvious disgust. "Sorry. Now where would you like to go for—?"

"Nowhere." Dennie scowled at him, disappointed on more counts than just missing Victoria. "If she's not here, I can't spare the time." She turned back to the revolving doors.

"Wait a minute." Alec caught her arm. "Where are you going? You have to eat. It's Friday. You need your energy for the weekend. And if you have to eat, it might as well be with—"

"You? No." Dennie disentangled her arm from his grasp. "Nothing personal, but if your aunt's not here, I've got to go back to the library. Thanks anyway."

"The library?" Alec followed her out the doors and into the street. "What are you doing at a library? Wait a minute."

"Alec, forget it." Dennie faced him, while people pushed past them. "You're a lot of fun, and you kiss very well, but I don't have time to toy with you now. I'm busy. Go play with somebody else."

Alec grabbed her arm as she turned away.

"Dinner. If you're skipping lunch, you're going to need dinner. I'll pay. I have—"

"I know. Plenty of money." Dennie frowned at him. "Will your aunt be there?"

"What is this with my aunt?" Alec frowned back at her.

"Will your aunt be there?" Dennie repeated with deliberate patience.

"Yes," Alec said. "If I have to drag her into the restaurant myself, my aunt will be there. I'll meet you at eight in the lobby. What do you say?"

"Fine. I would love to have dinner with you *and your aunt*. Now go away, I have to work." Dennie pulled her arm out of his grasp and turned down the street toward the university, and Alec watched her go.

She was going to a library? Alec turned the problem over in his mind. What the hell could there be in a library that would interest a con—?

Of course. His aunt was an academic, so Dennie would assume she'd published. She was looking up Aunt Vic's publications so she could dazzle her at dinner. Alec shook his head in admiration. Hell of a woman, that Dennie. It was almost a shame to arrest her. He turned back to the hotel to tell Harry there'd be two more at dinner. And if Dennie really was spending the afternoon at the library, that would give him time to run some checks and set up the next day. Really, she was just playing into his hands.

Alec thought of Dennie in his hands and grew warm. It really was a shame she was a crook. Then he shoved that thought away, too, and went to lay the groundwork for arresting her.

On her way back through the lobby after a very productive afternoon at the library, Dennie was waylaid by Baxter, the manager, looking even more rabbity than usual.

"Whatever it is, I didn't do it," Dennie said, trying to duck by him.

"She said you watched her give a speech today," Baxter said, trailing her with a hopeless expression.

Dennie stopped. "It was a public speech. I sat in the back. I'm not allowed at a public speech?"

"I tried to point that out," Baxter said, clearly

hoping one of the combatants would be on his side. "I asked if you tried to speak to her, and she said no but that wasn't the point." Now that he had Dennie's attention, he began to wax eloquent. "So then I said, 'But Mrs. Meredith, surely she's allowed in a public place,' and that seemed to make her angrier."

It was probably the "Mrs. Meredith," Dennie told him silently. Reminders of marriage would have been ill-timed. Baxter, meanwhile, droned on. There must be people at home who loved him very much if he was used to being listened to when he talked like this. Dennie could picture the children gathered round, and his thin little wife holding the latest baby, and maybe a little dog. Not like Walter, though. Walter would have peed on him out of exasperation by now.

"—So I told her I'd make sure you didn't get near her again this weekend," Baxter finished. "That's all right, isn't it? I mean, we agreed about the police and all, so I thought that would be all right with you. Isn't it?"

"Sure," Dennie said, sidling away again. "Listen, I have to go to dinner with some people who are not Janice Meredith, so I'm going now. Give my best to the family."

"What family?" Baxter said, but she'd already turned and was heading for the elevators. Baxter was the least of her troubles. She had to be intelligent and insightful for Victoria Prentice that night so Victoria would see that she was a serious writer and convince Janice to spill everything. . . .

Fat chance.

Just do it, she told herself. Thinking about it was only depressing.

At seven that night, Harry hefted the suitcase with the sound equipment in one hand while he knocked on Victoria's door with the other, wishing he could be anyplace else on the planet. She was a dangerous woman with dangerous eyes, and he'd been thinking about her since he'd seen her the night before. The best thing he could do would be to wire her and get out because—

Victoria opened the door in a white lace robe, and Harry lost his train of thought while he tried to keep his eyes on hers instead of looking down.

Her eyes were an incredibly soft brown, a sexy soft brown. . . . *Don't look at her at all,* he told himself and barged past her into the room which he suddenly noticed was dominated by a huge bed covered with a red damask spread. It wasn't any huger than most hotel beds, but somehow with Victoria in the room, it looked like a football field.

Forget the bed, he told himself and realized that all that was left to think about was either Victoria or the plan for that night. Easy choice.

"I have two main concerns about tonight," he said, staring past her shoulder when they were sitting at the desk in the corner of the room.

"Only two?" Victoria said.

She was impossible. "Concentrate," Harry said. "The first is entrapment. You have to let this guy come to you. Let him make all the suggestions. Don't make any moves yourself. And don't agree right away. Make him work for it."

Victoria put her chin in her hand and smiled at him. "You know my mother gave me this same advice when I started dating."

"Well, pay more attention to me than you did to your mother." Harry scowled at her, so annoyed, he forgot to avoid her. "If it looks like you encouraged him to swindle you, he can yell 'entrapment' and the case gets thrown out of court."

"All right," Victoria said. "I'm skeptical, right?"

Harry thought about it. Victoria was so sharp, she might actually scare Bond off. "You might get further being dizzy. You know, one of those women who can't concentrate long enough to make up their minds."

Victoria scowled at him. "No, I don't know one of those women who can't concentrate long enough to make up their minds."

Harry rolled his eyes. This was no time for her to be deliberately difficult. "Look, the longer we can string him along, the more time we have to gather evidence. If you're skeptical, he may get cold feet and think that you're having him investigated. And if he gets even a whiff that we're closing in on him, he'll be gone. If he just thinks you're too damn dumb to make a decision, he'll hang in there."

Victoria sighed. "All right. I'll play dumb."

"Thank you," Harry said, glaring at her.

"My pleasure," Victoria said, glaring back. "What's the second concern?"

Harry lost his train of thought again. Those soft brown eyes really sparkled when she glared. There was a lot of fire in Victoria. How the hell was she ever going to play dumb enough to fool Bond?

"Harry," Victoria repeated. "What's the second concern?"

"What?"

"You said you had two concerns," Victoria said, speaking slowly and clearly. "What . . . is . . . the . . . second . . . concern?"

"Oh," Harry said. "Bond finds out you're a setup and gets rid of you."

Victoria swallowed. "What exactly do you mean by 'gets rid of'?"

Harry's uneasiness solidified into frank doubt; he must have been out of his mind to think about involving Victoria in this. She could get hurt. The whole plan was out of the question. "Bond's never hurt anyone before, but we've got a hell of a lot on him. If we get him now, he won't see the outside again for some time. And even con men have been known to get violent when facing a lot of prison time—"

"Oh," Victoria said.

"—which is why I think this is a dumb idea," Harry went on as if she hadn't spoken. "I don't think this will work. I think we'd better count you out." He got up to go, relieved.

Victoria stayed seated. "Wait a minute. If I don't do it, who will? You?"

"No." Harry shook his head. "Nobody'd believe I'm a college professor. Alec can carry it by himself. He and that Banks woman are going to dinner with you anyway. Just let him handle it."

"But then Alec might get hurt," Victoria said.

"Well, it *is* his job," Harry pointed out. "It wouldn't be the first time he's taken a risk."

"It wouldn't?" Victoria said, visibly appalled. "I thought all he did was investigate fraud, like some sort of accountant-avenger. I thought the worst that could happen in his job was a paper cut."

"Uh, no," Harry said.

Victoria bit her lip. "I'll do it. I can't let Alec take all the risk."

Harry's heart sank. "Sure you can. It's his job."

"No." Victoria's voice was firm. "This will work a lot better if I do it. And you and Alec will be around all the time. How much danger can I be in?"

"I don't know," Harry said. "Any is too much."

"Why, Harry." Victoria smiled at him. "That's really sweet of you."

"The hell it is." Harry scowled at her, resisting that smile with every ounce of self-protecting skepticism he could muster. "Do you know how much trouble I'd be in if a civilian got bumped off while working undercover for me? I'm only seven years away from full retirement. I don't need this."

"Harry, do you really loathe me as much as you seem to?" Victoria asked, and Harry was caught flatfooted.

"No," he said. "What? No. What are you talking about?"

"You look at me as if I'm something that's going to bite." She looked up at him, sweet, confused, puzzled, adorable—

Harry caught himself. The hell she was

adorable. She was manipulating him. "You know damn well what's going on here," he blustered. "Business. And if you're going to play games, you're out."

"I never play games." Victoria stood up. "I just wanted to know where I stood with you."

Too close, that's where she stood. She was close enough that if he leaned forward, those soft white curls would tickle his cheek. He took a step back. "Right where you are is fine," he said. "If you're going through with this, get dressed."

The phone rang a little after seven, and Dennie draped herself across the bed to pick it up. "Hello?"

"Banks, is that you?"

"Hello, Taylor," Dennie said. "What do you want?"

"What the hell have you been doing?"

"What are you talking about?" Dennie made a face at the phone. "I'm on vacation. Leave me alone."

"The hell you are. You're doing something

Jennifer Crusie

because I've got about forty people on my butt warning me what they're going to do if you don't stay away from Janice Meredith. What the hell are you harassing a feminist for, anyway?"

Dennie froze, visions of her scoop disappearing before her eyes. If an ignoramus like Taylor had heard about it . . . "I don't know what you're talking about."

"You've been chasing her around some hotel lobby and watching her eat."

Dennie closed her eyes. Janice had set the bloodhounds on her even though she'd stayed away from her. This was one angry woman. "I just tried to talk to her. That's all, I swear."

"Well, stop it. She's got a lot of powerful friends. I mean it. If I get any more calls, you're fired."

Fired? Dennie's stomach did a fast plummet. She couldn't afford to get fired. She had to stay employed long enough to save enough money to quit. Walter's dog biscuits were not cheap. *He's bluffing,* she told herself. "Boy, Taylor, you really know how to back your reporters. Definitely a Pulitzer Prize–winning spine you've got there."

Taylor's voice rose to its usual shriek. "I didn't send you out on any Janice Meredith story, and I'll be damned if I'll take the heat for you for nothing. Now lay off or you're fired! Got it?"

Dennie swallowed. "Gotcha, Taylor. You're a real pro." She hung up on him, chilled by his threat. Journalism jobs weren't all that easy to get or she'd have jumped Taylor's ship a long time ago. And there was no doubt he'd fire her in a second if he thought his own job was in any danger. But she couldn't give up the interview; it was going to be too good. And it was a whole lot more than a story now, anyway; it was a quest. Something she had to do to prove she really was good, really was gutsy and brave and intelligent and—

Employed. Employed was necessary. How could she get this story without losing her job? *Stick with Alec,* she thought. Not even Janice Meredith could get her fired for dating an old friend's nephew.

Could she?

Sure, she could, but Alec was Dennie's only hope. If she was careful, surely she could get Victoria to support her. Surely Janice would understand.

Dennie winced and decided thinking about doing risky things was counterproductive. She should just dive straight in. Patience would. When they were little kids out on her uncle's farm in the summers, Patience was always the first one to jump into the pond. She'd stand on the ledge on the far side and yell, "Come on, Dennie," and Dennie would dip a toe in the shallow end and shake her head. Only after an hour of yelling and coaxing on Patience's part and watching and doubting on Dennie's part would Dennie actually stand on the ledge. "Come on, Dennie," Patience would repeat, the living embodiment of her name. "I'll catch you. Jump. It's great!" And Dennie would hold her nose and jump, and it would be great, except for the time she skinned her knee on a rock by jumping crooked, or the time she scraped her toe on the ledge and it bled, or the time she broke her arm—

But Patience had always been there to catch her. And now she wasn't. Patience was on her honeymoon so she wouldn't even be available for bail if Janice got Dennie arrested. A smart woman would pack her bags and head back to Taylor and safety.

Even while she had the thought, Dennie knew she wasn't going back. Before, she'd been doing a too-easy job without realizing it. Now, she knew. If she went back without the interview, she'd be a failure, even if it was only to herself and Walter. She had to go on, even if she lost her job. Even if she got arrested for stalking. Even if Patience wasn't there. She was going to have to jump.

"Right," she said and went to get dressed, but her fingers fumbled with the zipper, and she finally leaned her head against the mirror and took deep breaths until she was reasonably calm again.

Risking was turning out to be a very depressing business.

While Victoria was in the bathroom dressing, Harry unpacked the briefcase, arranging the equipment on the desk so that when she came back everything would be ready. Now that she was gone, he noticed her perfume faintly. It wasn't flowery at all, more spicy with a hint of something else. It made him nervous, and he fiddled with a microphone until one of the pieces dropped off. Damn good thing he always had spares. Cautious, that was him. Nothing to worry about. He was in control.

Victoria came out of the bathroom and said, "All right, how do we do this?"

Her dress was made of a rosy slippery material that sort of fell over her, Harry noticed. He also noticed that Victoria was trim in some places and full in others; this was a dress that didn't leave much to the imagination.

He shook his head, trying to stomp on his own imagination. "Nope."

"What do you mean, 'nope'?" Victoria put her hands on her hips. "This is a great dress."

"You can see everything in that dress," Harry said.

"So what are you, my mother?" Victoria asked.

"No," Harry said. "I'm the man who has to hide stereo equipment on you. Got anything that doesn't fit like Saran Wrap?"

Victoria slid open the closet door. "Be my guest."

Harry went to paw through her clothes. Her perfume wafted out of the closet as he shoved hangers back and forth. She brought more clothes for a weekend in a hotel than he had in his closet back home. That was a woman for you. Good thing he didn't have to share a closet with her. He clamped down on his thoughts again. "Here," he said finally, pulling a heavy jacket and skirt out, and Victoria looked at him as if he were insane.

"Harry, that's a day suit. It's seven-thirty in the evening. I can't wear a tweed suit to dinner. He would think I was strange."

"Lots of people wear tweed suits to dinner at night," Harry said.

"Yes, and they're all men."

"No, they're not," Harry began, and Victoria put her hand on his arm and moved him to one side so she could slide hangers back and forth. He checked his sleeve to see if her hand had left a mark; it felt as if it had left a mark.

"How about this?" She pulled out a black dress.

Harry felt the fabric. "Don't you wear anything stiff?"

"No," Victoria said. "I'm against stiff." She grinned. "In fabric anyway."

Harry handed her the dress. "Go put this on and don't talk dirty."

"You know you have a *lot* in common with my mother," Victoria said, but she took the dress back in the bathroom with her.

When she was gone, Harry told himself she was impossible. Then he grinned in spite of himself.

When she came out, the black dress was draped looser, but it was also lower in front and back so a lot more Victoria showed.

"I don't know," Harry said, trying to look someplace there wasn't skin.

"Harry, just wire me up. We're running out of time here."

Harry stared at her dress, frowning. How the hell was he going to get everything taped and hidden in that dress?

Finally, Victoria said, *"What?"*

"I'm used to taping this onto guys in shirts," he said. "I guess I'll just tape this lower."

Victoria's eyebrows went up. "Tape?"

Harry grinned. "What are you worried about? A little tape? Hell, if you had chest hair, you'd have something to worry about."

"Chest hair?"

"It really hurts when you rip tape off chest hair."

Victoria crossed her arms and glared at him until he relented.

"We'll tape the microphone to your . . . uh, ribs," he said. "You can do that part. The transmitter goes to your side, sort of. Really, it's no big deal."

"All right," Victoria said. "What do I do first?"

"Unzip your dress," Harry said.

"Why, Harry," Victoria said. "You impetuous fool."

"God knows how you've lived this long without somebody killing you," Harry said. "Will you just unzip?"

"Your technique needs work," Victoria said, but she turned around and unzipped her dress.

Harry watched the zipper slide down showing a lot of Victoria's creamy flesh, some of it covered with black lace. "You can stop," he said, trying to keep his voice from cracking. "That's far enough." He picked up the microphone. "This is the mike. Tape this under your . . . ribs on the right side, not too near your heart." He held out the mike to her.

She turned around. "Harry, this is dumb. We're two adults, doing a job. You'd see more of me in a bathing suit." She made a swift shrugging motion with her shoulders, and the top of her dress fell off over her arms, and she stood there, curvy and warm in black lace, and Harry told himself not to have a heart attack. "Just tape it where you want it," she said, and he forced his mind back to the technical problem at hand.

"Don't undress in front of men, Vic," he said to cover his confusion. "It's dangerous."

"Vic?"

Harry tried not to look at her. "Got it from Alec. It suits you better than Victoria. Victoria's feminine." And so was she, standing there in front of him, half dressed. If he worked with her much longer, he'd lose his mind.

Victoria glared at him. "Thank you."

He ripped a strip of the tape off with a lot more force than was necessary and pressed the microphone to the lace under her right breast, trying very hard not to linger there any longer than he absolutely had to. It took him a lot longer than he thought it would. Then he taped the wire around the curve of her back and fastened the transmitter over her right hip. He smoothed the tape against the lace that was warm from her flesh and cursed steadily under his breath the whole time.

"There," he snarled finally. "Put your dress back on."

She was unusually silent as she dressed, and he felt ashamed. "Uh, I'm sorry," he said. "Listen, don't worry about tonight. I'll be listening from the kitchen. I'll be there."

"Good," she said. "I have to put my makeup on now. Maybe you'd better go."

"Makeup?" he said, puzzled. "You look great. You don't need any more makeup."

"Go away," Victoria said. "I'll see you downstairs."

"No, you won't," Harry said. "I'll be in the

kitchen." But he left anyway, delighted to be out of danger and feeling curiously bereft and annoyed at the same time.

Dangerous woman, that Vic.

When Harry was gone, Victoria sat down for a moment to try to gather the thoughts that Harry had sent south when he touched her.

Because Harry was definitely not someone she wanted to be thinking about the way she was thinking about him. All right, sure, he was big and broad, and he had nice hands, well, great hands, and he was fun to tease, and he wasn't boring at all, but still . . .

Harry?

There was no way. She'd worked all her life to get where she was now, carefully choosing the right men who wouldn't get in the way of her career and just as carefully kissing them good-bye when it turned out she'd misjudged them. And now she was at the top of her field, tenured, respected. People were making noises about the college presidency, how perfect she'd be for the job. Harry would not fit in.

Victoria thought about Harry in the middle of the college political circuit and smiled in spite of herself. Harry would probably do damn well there. In fact, she couldn't imagine any place Harry wouldn't do damn well. That was one of the many things she found so attractive about him. That and his shoulders and his hands and—

Oh, hell, she thought. *I'm sixty-two years old, and I'm still falling for the wrong men. When will I learn?*

Then she put Harry firmly from her mind and went to finish her makeup.

When Alec found Harry in the hotel kitchen, he was hunched over the recorder, snarling about Victoria.

"Aunt Vic can handle this," Alec told him. "This guy isn't dangerous. There's no problem."

"She'll spook him." Harry was even grouchier than usual. "That woman is a mental case. She'll get herself killed."

Alec frowned at him, bewildered. "Will you relax? She's the smartest woman I know. She didn't get to the top of her profession by being nuts."

"I don't like it," Harry grouched. "And as far as I'm concerned, she is nuts. Can't you control her?"

Alec laughed. "Control Aunt Vic? Good luck. The best you can do is aim her. Will you relax?" Harry snarled again, and Alec gave up. "I have to go meet Dennie," he said. "Try not to chew on the tape recorder during dinner. It's government issue."

Alec almost missed Dennie when she got off the elevator. She was wearing a black linen dress with a standup collar and long sleeves, and she'd pulled her hair back in a knot on her neck. "What is this?" he asked her as she came toward the gilt chairs where he was sitting. "You dressing for the convent now?"

Dennie looked uncertain for the first time since he'd met her. "Sorry. I'm trying to look serious and trustworthy." The lilt was gone from her voice, and she seemed diminished somehow.

"Hey, it's all right." Alec stood up, alarmed. "I'm sorry. Really. Come on, fight back here. Don't go all weak on me."

"Things aren't going well for me," Dennie said. "My boss yelled at me. I'm a little depressed. Give me a minute."

Her boss had yelled? That rat Bond. She looked crushed, and Alec hated it. It was going to be a pleasure to arrest *him*. "Come here." Alec took her hand and pulled her down beside him.

"I remember these chairs." Dennie looked around as she sank into one. "I was threatened with arrest here yesterday."

"Arrest?" Alec felt his heart skip a beat. Was somebody else after her too? It took him a moment to realize that he wasn't afraid somebody else would get his collar, it was that if somebody else moved in on Bond, he wouldn't be able to protect her. Just when he'd decided to protect her, he wasn't certain, but the idea had him in full grip now.

"I'm probably going to lose my job too." Dennie shook her head. "I'm going to bounce back from this, I really am. It's just taking me a minute."

"You know if your job involves doing something you'll get arrested for, you might want to rethink careers," Alec said, adding silently, *especially since I don't want to be the one who busts you.*

Dennie shrugged. "Oh, heck, what's a jail sentence? At least I'll have three square meals." She looked at him plaintively. "Will you bring Walter to visit me in the slammer?"

"Hell, I'll bail you out for conjugal visits." Alec put his arm around her and pulled her close, patting her shoulder. "You're just depressed because you look like a nun. It depresses me too."

"I know this is a tough one," Dennie said, more to herself than to Alec, "but I need it. I need to know I can get the really tough ones. Even if I go to jail."

"If it's that bad, I strongly suggest a career change. Depressing careers are bad for you. Also,

I think your hair's pulled back too tight." Alec pushed her head forward and started pulling bobby pins out of the knot. "It's got to be giving you a headache. It's giving me a headache."

"It's not that bad." Dennie put her chin in her hands and stared into the lobby while he unpinned her hair. "I thought it made me look more stable."

"It made you look like Nurse Ratched." Alec pulled the last pin out and watched her hair fall down into tangled silky curls. He pulled his fingers through it, partly to even out the tangles and partly because he knew it would feel so good against his fingers. Dennie never moved. "You know you're pretty passive here. Would this be a good time for me to make my move?"

"Not if you want to keep your teeth," Dennie said, but there was no threat in her voice.

"Hey," Alec said again, and pulled her back to face him. "Whatever it is, it can't be that bad. I'm here. I'll help. Come on." He leaned forward and kissed her on the forehead and then on the nose and then, softly, against his better judgment, on the mouth.

"Don't do that," Dennie said, her voice cracking. "You're just a cog in my career wheel. Don't try to get important to me."

"Of course not," Alec said, and then he had to kiss her again, still softly but this time with some staying power. "Feel free to toy with me and then cast me aside," he whispered against her mouth, and kissed her again, feeling her lips finally move against his and her hands rest lightly on his arms.

People were staring, he noticed vaguely as he came up for air. Probably envious. He'd have been envious. He leaned forward to take her mouth again but she pulled back. "Do you think I'm a loser?"

"Well, I didn't until you started acting like one," Alec said, and Dennie dropped her hands and straightened.

"That was cruel," she said, some of the flash back in her eyes.

"Probably dumb too," Alec said. "If I'd stuck with being understanding, I might have gotten laid in gratitude."

"Oh, yeah, I bet you get a lot of sex that way,"

Dennie said, all of the flash coming back. "On account of you being so sensitive and all."

"Good," Alec said. "Now tell me I'm ugly, and I'll take you into dinner and introduce you to my aunt Vic."

Dennie grinned at him with such warmth, he was rocked by it. "And then you'll buy me ice cream, right? You are a nice guy, Alec."

"Well, don't tell anybody." Alec stood up to keep from reaching for her again. "The last thing I want is for somebody to think I'm one of those sensitive nineties kind of guys."

"Don't worry," Dennie said, standing too. "Nobody thinks you're sensitive."

"Good."

"Except me."

"Knock it off," Alec said, and pulled her toward the dining room.

Harry sat in the kitchen and listened to Victoria pretending to be a half-wit while they waited for Alec and the Banks woman to join them. He enjoyed it enormously.

This is some woman, he told himself. Tough. Bright. Brave. Smart. Soft. Good thing he had fifty-eight years of experience to protect him or he might have fallen for her. Good thing he was too smart for that.

He heard Vic say, "So this would be an investment in my future. Oh, Mr. Bondman, that sounds very . . . good. Really." Then he heard her pause and add in a soft, slightly confused voice, "Did you say this was in Florida?"

Bond must be ready to throttle her. They wouldn't need to send him up the river. They could just let Vic drive him crazy. He started to laugh, and then he remembered her in black lace and stopped.

Oh, hell.

Whatever was bothering Dennie hadn't gone away, Alec realized. It just metamorphosed into something different: antagonism toward Brian Bond.

Alec introduced her to Victoria, Donald, and Bond, and watched her charm the daylights out of them all, especially Victoria. She really was amazing once she got her sights on someone. Witty and intelligent, she drew Victoria out all through dinner, asking her about her career and discussing her paper from that morning with clarity and understanding. Alec gave her another point for thoroughness: He loved his aunt and even he hadn't sat through three academic papers for her, but Dennie had. Hell of a woman.

"You came to hear my paper this morning?" Victoria had said, clearly flattered but fortunately still pretending to be a half-wit.

"I actually went to hear Janice Meredith," Dennie said. "But I stayed to hear yours when I saw your name in the program. Alec had told me so much about you, and obviously he hadn't exaggerated."

"Alec told you about my research?" Victoria asked, flabbergasted.

"Certainly. He's very proud of you," Dennie said.

Alec opened his mouth to comment, and Dennie kicked him under the table. "Ouch," he said, and glared at her.

"I notice you've done a lot of work on Shakespeare and pop literature." Dennie leaned forward, and Victoria did too. "I also thought your article on *Much Ado* as a forties screwball comedy was fascinating."

"That article was in *Signs* two years ago." Victoria looked at Dennie in disbelief.

"I know," Dennie said. "I read it this afternoon at the library."

Attagirl, Alec thought, and then remembered she was one of the bad guys.

Victoria transferred her gaze to Alec. "Since when do you date women who go to libraries?"

"Hey," Alec said. "I have taste. I know a winner when I see one." He smiled goofily at Dennie. "Right, honey?"

Dennie ignored him to concentrate on Victoria's publishing history while Victoria nattered on about nothing. Bond and Donald listened politely and then began to talk quietly to themselves.

Alec shifted in his chair. Something was very wrong. If Dennie was on Bond's team, she should be working the conversation around to real estate by now. Hell, if she hadn't been there, Bond could have brought it up; that had to be what he was talking about with Donald now. After all, that's why they were all having dinner together. Alec bowed to no one in his respect for Dennie's deviousness, but for the life of him, he couldn't see how she was going to move the conversation from feminist literary criticism to Florida oceanfront property.

After another fifteen minutes and the salad, it became obvious that she wasn't.

"So, Brian," Alec said, breaking into Dennie's discussion of *Thelma & Louise* as the nineties version of *The Awakening*. "My aunt tells me you have some pretty exciting land deals cooking. Tell me about it. I'm always interested in a good investment, especially real estate." He flashed his standard goofy grin. "Can't go wrong with real estate."

"What?" Dennie said, momentarily thrown off stride.

"Well," Bond said modestly, "I wouldn't want to exaggerate the possibilities, but—"

"Absolutely phenomenal," Donald pronounced. "Alec, you really should get a piece of this."

"You think so?" Alec said, trying to look slow but interested at the same time. God bless Donald for suggesting it.

"Think how cute it would be," Victoria cooed. "We could get adjacent lots. Like the Kennedy compound."

"The Prentice compound," Alec said. "I like it. Tell me more, Brian."

Brian told him more all through dinner. Victoria grew girlishly excited, Donald remained proprietarily pleased, and Alec did his best to become cautiously enthusiastic.

What he didn't notice in time was that Dennie was losing her temper.

"Let me get this straight," she said to Bond finally as the dessert plates were being set before them. "You're selling oceanfront property that the EPA says cannot be developed, but you're sure that they'll reverse that decision after a little political pressure?"

Bond shrugged urbanely. "You have to understand Washington, my dear. The Beltway does things differently."

"Oh, absolutely," Donald said.

"That's the dumbest thing I've ever heard," Dennie said, and Alec jerked around to face her, appalled.

"Dennie!" he said, and Victoria chimed in with, "Dennie, dear!" but she plunged on, ignoring them both.

"Al Gore is in Washington," she told Bond, disdain palpable in her voice. "Have you read his book? The only thing he's more protective of than endangered coastline is Tipper's butt. There's no way—"

In desperation, Alec knocked his glass of wine into her lap, but he forgot Dennie's reflexes. Her hand shot out to block it, the glass overbalanced, and the dark red wine splashed down his pale blue shirtfront instead.

Alec stood up. "Well, gotta go," he said, blotting the wine from his chest with a napkin while he used his other hand to jerk Dennie to her feet. "We'll just go back to the room and try to get this out. Say good night, Dennie."

"Wait a minute!" Dennie said, but Alec stiff-armed her from the dining room while Victoria's good-bye bubbled behind them.

Chapter 5

Once they were out in the lobby, Dennie jerked herself out of his grasp and stalked toward the elevator.

"Now, wait a minute," Alec said, but she kept on walking. He moved after her, taking long strides to catch up with her at the elevator doors.

"Go away," she said, and he grabbed her arm and pulled her around.

"What's wrong with you?" he said.

"What's wrong with *me*?" She jerked her arm back again. "I finally get to meet your aunt, and things are going great, I'm going to *save* her, and

136

you try to dump wine all over me! What's wrong with *you*?"

"Why is my aunt so important?" Alec asked. "And why were you giving Bondman such a hard time?"

"Your aunt is important because she can get me an interview I need," Dennie said. "Well, also because she's a sweetie, but the interview too. And Bondman is a crook. I can't believe you can't see that. Anybody could spot him a mile away, but not you. No, you're offering him money. The Prentice compound. What a twit you are!"

Alec frowned at her. "What interview? You're a reporter?" He shook his head, but he felt happier than any time since he'd met her. "You know, I don't think it's a good idea for women to have careers. I mean, look at you. You're so wrapped up in yours, you're knocking over wineglasses and suspecting innocent real estate salesmen of fraud. It would probably be a good thing if you got fired."

Dennie became dangerously still. "A good thing."

"Sure. What was that you were yapping about yesterday? The importance of failing. And now look at you, a failure in the making. Just what you wanted." He beamed at her.

"A failure. I'm a failure? I almost had it all, and you ruined it! You *rat*!" Dennie swung at him with her soft little purse, and Alec ducked.

"I love a woman with spunk," he said, and her elbow caught him by accident on the backswing, connecting solidly with his nose, which started to bleed.

"Ouch," he said, "Oh, hell." He began searching his pockets for a handkerchief, trying to keep his head tilted up while the blood dripped down his shirt and mingled with the wine stains.

"I don't believe this." Dennie opened her purse. "Here." She handed him a fistful of Kleenex, and then punched the elevator button. "A million guys in this city, and I have to hit a bleeder."

"Anybody bleeds if you hit him on the nose," Alec said nasally, trying to stanch the flow. "Even if he gets hit with a limp punch like yours."

The elevator doors opened, and she pulled him in and put her arm around his shoulders as the door closed. "Lean back. We have to stop this bleeding before you drown in it. What floor are you on?"

He leaned back, his head against the elevator wall. "We better go to your room. Mine's a mess."

"There's no way," she began, and then stopped. Alec tried to drop his head to see what she was up to, and she pushed his forehead back farther, jamming his head into the wall. "All right," she said. "My room." She punched the button for her floor.

"You know, I never thought of you as Florence Nightingale." He tried to straighten his head again. "You're more the Lady Macbeth type."

She jammed his head back again. "I never thought of you as Pee-wee Herman, but that's who you sound like."

God, she was exasperating. "If I don't bleed to death, I may kill you."

"How? You get close, I'll hit you in the nose again."

"I'll wait until your guard is down." Alec raised his head cautiously, shoving her hand away when she tried to push him back again. The bleeding had stopped.

"My guard is never down." She peered at him

to see if he was all right, and he kissed her. When she pulled back, he held her face between his hands.

"I need a nurse," he said to her. "Somebody to stay with me all night and make sure I don't bleed to death."

"Fat chance," she said. "You're disgusting."

The doors opened at the seventh floor.

"We'll talk about it," he said. "Where's your room? You can help clean me up."

"Good idea." Dennie pushed past him to lead the way. "A little water and you'll be cleaned off and I can throw you out."

"You really sound like Lady Macbeth," he said as he followed her.

"Yes, and look what happened to her." Dennie shook her head. "And all because she married a monomaniac."

"Oh, so everything was Macbeth's fault. Hey, she wanted it too."

"Wanted what?" Dennie stopped at her door and shoved in her room card.

"All those crimes in the dark." Alec moved beside her. "She wanted them too."

He grinned down at her, and she pushed him away to open the door to her room.

"Once you're clean, you're gone."

"Absolutely," Alec lied.

"I think this sounds wonderful," Victoria burbled up at Brian as they left the table. She'd only had dessert to undo Dennie's damage, and it hadn't been easy. Bond had been much quieter after Dennie and Alec had gone, telling Donald that perhaps the dinner table wasn't the best place to discuss business. *It's the perfect place*, Victoria wanted to say, *Harry's listening*, but she backed off and entertained Brian and Donald with the most fatuous conversation she could think of, repeating everything she'd ever heard Trella say. By the time they'd stood to leave the table, both men were relaxed again. "And please don't let little Dennie upset you. She's very protective of us all, especially of Alec. I'm sure once you explain it again, she'll understand."

"She just doesn't understand how things work in Washington," Donald said beside her, and

Victoria felt warm toward him for the first time because he was such a bona fide twit and was therefore making her act look so much better.

"And I just love the idea of the Prentice compound," Victoria burbled on. "You really should talk to Alec later. Do you think you could meet him sometime?"

"Of course," Bond said, but he still looked wary.

"The bar at eleven," Donald said automatically. "Where we met last night. What do you say?"

I say "God bless Donald," Victoria thought, and Bond seemed to feel the same.

"I'll call Alec and tell him," Victoria promised. "Now you two go ahead and talk business. I'll just go back to my room and call Alec."

"Don't forget, we're having dinner tomorrow to celebrate the deal," Donald said roguishly. "Maybe we'll have to call it the Compton-Prentice compound."

"You never know," Victoria twinkled back at him, and thought, *Over my dead body*. There were some things she was not willing to do to fight crime, and marrying Donald topped the list.

"This is great," Alec told Dennie as she mopped off his face in her bathroom. "Nobody's washed my face for me since I was ten."

"Who hit you when you were ten?" Dennie moved his nose cautiously back and forth.

"Ouch! What are you doing?"

"Seeing if it's broken."

He caught her hand and pulled it away. "It's not broken. You didn't hit me hard enough to break it."

"Well, you bled like a stuck pig."

"Noses always bleed like that." He stood up and took off his jacket.

"What are you doing?"

"I'm covered with blood." He unbuttoned his shirt. Really, it was logical. Anybody would take off his clothes if they were covered in blood and wine.

Too bad he hadn't bled on her.

"And what do you think you're going to change

into here?" Dennie stood with her hands on her hips, looking at him with disgust, which was not the reaction he'd been hoping for. She was exasperating and infuriating and impossible, and he'd never wanted a woman more, especially now that it seemed entirely probable that she wasn't a crook after all. He'd been feeling positively cheerful ever since she'd snarled at Bond.

And the night was not over yet.

He ran cold water in the sink and dropped his shirt in it. "You've got to get blood out fast or it stains. And then there's the wine." He turned off the water. "You know—out, out, damned spot. Now what shall we do while my shirt soaks?"

She folded her arms and looked at him grimly.

No go, he thought. *Well, let's lull her into a false sense of security.*

"Room service hot fudge sundaes." Alec moved past her to the phone. "We didn't get dessert."

Dennie watched him dial room service and then went back in the bathroom to scrub his shirt and think, leaving the door open so she could hear if he called anybody else. She listened to him order the sundaes, and then she soaped the stains on his shirt and let her mind run on with the idea she'd had in the elevator, the idea that had made her decide that bringing Alec back to the room was a good idea.

Alec was not stupid but he was acting stupid.

Victoria Prentice was not stupid but she was acting dumber than Alec.

They were both fascinated with this Bondman creature who was clearly selling land they weren't going to be able to develop.

Therefore they were up to something. At the moment, Dennie didn't care if it was legal or illegal; all she cared about was that it was a story. And she'd been on the inside of it and blown it by shooting off her big mouth.

The only way she could get back in was by pumping Alec and his aunt. And by talking to Bondman.

She rinsed the shirt again and then wrung it out. The stains were fainter but still there. Alec would have to send it to the cleaners.

But first he'd have to talk with her.

She came out of the bedroom just as the room service arrived, and smiled at Alec while he signed for the desserts.

"This was a great idea," she told him and took one of the sundaes. She sat on the edge of the bed and dipped her spoon into the whipped cream and licked it off, watching him flinch. That was another good thing about Alec: He was easy to turn on. Maybe she should seduce him for the information.

Alec picked up his ice cream and ignored her, stretching out on the bed to watch the old TV movie he'd turned on while she'd been in the bathroom. He looked long and lanky, and his chest was broad and lightly furred in the lamplight, and he was infinitely desirable. She felt the room grow warmer and shifted a little on the bed.

Maybe she shouldn't seduce him. She should probably stick with things she could control. She licked hot fudge from her spoon, and Alec watched her again and clenched his teeth. Good. He was still distracted. She swung her legs up on the bed and stretched out. "You're awfully quiet," she told him around her hot fudge. "How's your nose?"

"It hurts," he said, looking pathetic, probably hoping for sympathy.

"Good. Think twice before you annoy me again."

"You're a bully." He scooped up some fudge and ice cream from his own sundae.

She watched him wince again as he ate. Maybe that wasn't from lust. Maybe it was from his almost-broken nose. "I am sorry if it really still hurts."

"How sorry are you?" He leered and wiggled his eyebrows.

"Not that sorry."

He laughed. "I like you, Dennie Banks. You're my kind of woman."

"Me and every other woman you meet," she sniffed, but she felt a little sizzle go up her spine, just the same. *Back to work, Banks.* "Speaking of people you've met, where did you find Bondman?"

"My aunt found him," Alec said, his eyes back on the screen. "Actually, the guy she's dating found him, and then the relationship spread."

"Do you really believe what he says?" Dennie asked, trying to keep the scorn out of her voice.

"Do I think Washington is corrupt? Hell, yes." Alec gestured at the screen. "They don't make them like this anymore."

Dennie squinted at the TV. A guy in a white lab coat was talking to three other guys in suits, and they were all frowning with concern. "That's because they made ten million of them back then. Monster picture, right?"

"Do not trash an entire genre," Alec said. "Monster movies have a long and honorable history." A close-up of the guy in the lab coat showed him still looking disturbed. Evidently he had only one facial expression. "Of course, this probably isn't one of the better examples," Alec said finally. "But still . . ."

Dennie put her half-finished sundae on the bedside table between them and leaned forward to see the screen better. "Is that Peter Cushing?"

"Very good," Alec said, and swapped his empty sundae glass for her half-full one.

"Hey," Dennie said, and Alec moved over to sit

beside her on the bed, shoving her over with his hip.

"You snooze, you lose." Alec spooned up some more hot fudge. "You can still have some. Your spoon's still in the dish."

It wasn't the lack of a spoon that was causing Dennie problems, it was Alec's proximity. The warmth from his kiss at the door last night came back, multiplied by how sweet he'd been kissing her in the lobby before dinner and bolstered by the fact that he was in the middle of a great story she wanted. He leaned next to her, half naked, warm wherever his body touched hers, and she vividly regretted giving up men. Actually, she'd had no trouble giving up other men, but giving up Alec, even though she'd never had him, that was a shame.

"Did I ever tell you my fantasy about whipped cream?" Alec asked her as he ate the last of hers.

Dennie's pulse kicked up at the thought. "If I had any interest in your fantasies, they wouldn't be fantasies," she said as coldly as she could while her entire body heated.

"That's harsh."

"Fran Lebowitz said it first."

"Good for her. Can we get back to my fantasy now?"

"No." Dennie dipped her spoon in the hot fudge and licked it, which made her think of other things, which was bad. Change of subject. "What *is* this movie?"

"*Island of Terror.* Science fiction from the sixties. A classic."

"You're kidding." Something moved on the TV screen, and Dennie gaped. "What is *that*?"

Alec stretched to put the sundae dish down and on the way back he just happened to put his arm around her. Before she could say anything, he said, "That's the alien life-form on the island. Haven't you been watching?"

Dennie leaned forward to see better and to keep herself from jumping him. "It looks like a big turtle."

"Their special effects budget must have been small," Alec said charitably.

Dennie looked skeptical. "That's a special effect?"

"For this movie, that's a special effect. Now

lean back and pay attention." He tightened his hold on her, and she leaned back into him. *This is a mistake,* she thought, but if it was, it was at least going to be a mistake that felt great. "This is where the movie gets scary, and the aliens attack," Alec went on. "You better hold on to me. Girls get scared easier than guys."

Dozens of turtles moved slowly across the beach, and Dennie began to laugh. The turtles were ridiculous, and Alec's arm was solid and warm. Life was suddenly getting better.

He held her close. "Hysterical from terror, huh?" He kissed her on the top of her head, and she thought dangerous thoughts.

Remember the job, she told herself, and tilted her head back and smiled at him. "I'm still mad at you, but since I'm quite sure you're going to set me up for breakfast tomorrow with your aunt, I might forgive you."

Alec looked disappointed but he coped. "Anything you want. Now pay attention to the movie." He tightened his arm around her some more. "Hey, do I know how to show a girl a good time or what? We'll have to come here often."

"I don't know." She shook her head, and her curls brushed his bare skin and made them both shiver. "This movie will be a tough one to top."

"Nonsense," Alec said, his voice cracking a little. "There's *The Blob. Plan 9 from Outer Space. I Was a Teenage Werewolf.* Dozens of classics."

"Oh, good." Against all her better judgment, she nestled down next to him. "I'll become a film connoisseur."

His arm tightened on her still more. "No, you won't. This isn't film. This is the movies."

The turtles advanced on the scientist's daughter, who turned and ran screaming.

Dennie tried to keep her attention on the movie. "Why is she running?"

"Because the men in the audience are tired of looking at turtles."

"Ah. An artistic decision." Dennie watched the turtles for a while, the least sexy thing in the room. "Actually, they kind of grow on you after a while," she said, and looked up at him. "I don't suppose there's a hope in hell that they actually get the scientist's daughter?"

"None," Alec said, and bent and kissed her while she was smiling up at him.

She should have moved away at once, should have just slid away, but that would have been dumb, to move away from all that heat and to stop the shudder he'd started in her. His tongue tickled her lips, and she opened to him, and he made her shudder again as he eased her back onto the bed. She moved under him as he pulled her close, curling into him, clutching at him as his hands moved over her. He slid his hand to the top of her zipper, and she thought, *Thank God, he'll be touching me soon,* and then the phone rang.

"Ignore it," Alec whispered thickly in her ear, but it rang again, just enough to remind Dennie that she had work to do. She had to find Bondman, she had to call Victoria to set up breakfast, she had to have Alec right now. . . .

No.

Dennie shoved him gently to one side and reached over him for the phone. "I told you," she said, a little breathlessly. "Career first."

Alec fell back on the bed. "I hate women's lib."

"Hello?" Dennie said.

"Dennie, dear," Victoria said. "Is Alec with you?"

"Right here, Victoria." Dennie turned to look at Alec beside her and regretting it instantly because he looked so good.

"Thank you *very* much," Alec called in the direction of the phone. "Hell of a time to call."

"Could I speak to him, dear? I've been calling his room for over an hour. Very frustrating."

"Believe me, I understand," Dennie said, trying to think cool, non-Alec thoughts. "Oh, before I hand the phone over, do you think we could have breakfast tomorrow? I'd love to talk. . . ."

"Well, I suppose—" Victoria began, sounding a little taken aback.

Dennie moved in for the kill. "You can? Oh, that's terrific. About ten in the Ivy Room? I can't wait. Here's Alec."

Dennie handed the phone over, and Alec sat up. "Hello, Aunt Vic," he said. "Don't ever call here again."

Dennie leaned closer and heard Victoria say, "Caught you in the middle of things, did I? Shame on you."

"How did you find me?" Alec pulled away a little, and Dennie took the hint and rolled off the bed. As she headed for the bathroom, she heard him say, "Better yet, *why* did you find me?"

Dennie checked his shirt and stayed close to the bathroom door to eavesdrop. "You can forget the Prentice compound," she heard him say. "Why would I want to live next door to you for the rest of my life? I'd never get laid again."

Then he listened for a while, and Dennie gave up and came out of the bathroom, holding his damp shirt and jacket.

"Looks like that shouldn't be a problem," Alec was saying gloomily. "See you in fifteen, Bond at eleven." He hung up and, as Dennie came toward him, said casually, "You know, many women manage to combine high-powered careers *and* great sex."

"Not this weekend," Dennie said, dumping the clothes in his lap so that he winced when the cold, damp fabric hit his skin. Good. If he cooled off, maybe she would too.

"Right," he said and stood to go. "Let me know if you ever get to the top and decide to unwind."

She smiled up at him, really sorry they didn't have time for each other and really glad he was leaving so her vision would clear and she'd stop breathing so heavily. "You'll be the first to know," she said.

Harry knocked on Victoria's door at ten-thirty. She answered it, still dressed from dinner.

"Are you alone?" he hissed at her angrily.

"Of course, I'm alone," she whispered back, and pulled him into the room. "Alec will be here any min—" she began in her normal voice, but then Harry cut her off.

"Who was the stiff?"

"What stiff?"

"The goon who wants to buy you a condo in the Keys," Harry said, scowling at her. "Where did he come from?"

"Connecticut," Victoria said, puzzled. "I told you about him. He's the one who got Bond for us. His name is Donald Compton. He teaches—"

"How do you know he's not in on the scam

with Bond?" Harry began to pace. "Where did he *come* from?"

"I told you. Connecticut. And I've known him for years." Victoria watched him stomp up and down the room. "Will you stop it? There's no problem. Donald's such a fool, he fell for Bond on his own, that's all. He's good for us. Camouflage."

"What's he buying you a condo for?" Harry stopped pacing and glared at her.

Victoria glared back. "He's not. He just thinks he is. It's his idea for the week. Next week, he'll want a ranch in Texas."

"With you on horseback."

"I don't do horseback. What is this?"

"Nothing," Harry said. "Just stay away from him."

"Harry!" Victoria said, but then Alec knocked on the door and she went to let him in. Harry would just have to solve his own problems, which looked to her like simple jealousy. There was a ridiculous idea. She smiled at the thought, and then kicked herself for smiling, taking her exasperation at Harry and at herself out on Alec.

"What are you so happy about?" Victoria asked

him when he was with them by the table, all smiles. "You were wrong. That nice Dennie is not a crook. We're having breakfast tomorrow."

"That's what he's so happy about," Harry growled, still glowering at everyone, "and that's because he's not thinking. Did it ever occur to you," he said to Alec, "that it might be a double play?"

"Yes." Alec's smile faded. "But I dismissed the thought because it was low and suspicious of me."

"What's a double play?" Victoria said, looking from one to the other. "Dennie tried to save me. I *like* her."

"Yes, and that makes you trust her," Harry said in disgust. "And when you're all pals, she says, 'Oh, I know all about real estate, so I can get you a *real* deal.' Then she and Bond walk off with your money. I can't believe how gullible you two are." He glanced at Victoria and then looked away. "At least, I can't believe how gullible Alec is."

"I don't believe it," Victoria said.

"Then why was she so anxious to meet you?" Harry asked. "She's practically been stalking you. She wants to have breakfast with you. Why?"

"Maybe because I'm fascinating?" Victoria said, exasperated.

"No, that's not it." Harry turned away before she could say anything else. "We can't trust her." He narrowed his eyes at Alec. "You didn't tell her anything, did you?"

"No." Alec sat on the edge of the table, feeling depressed again. "Which tells you how open and trusting I am."

"Good for you," Harry said.

"Shame on you," Victoria said.

"Forget her," Harry said, "and concentrate on Bond. You're going to be buying some real estate tomorrow. String him along for tonight. Tell him you need the night to think it over. Don't move too fast—"

"Harry, I've been doing this most of my adult life," Alec said, glowering now himself. "This I know how to do."

"I still don't believe Dennie is involved in this," Victoria said stubbornly.

"I don't know what I believe," Alec said. "Except that it's quarter to eleven, so I believe I'll have another drink. In the bar with Bond." He stood and bent to kiss Victoria's cheek. "Sleep tight and don't spill the beans at breakfast."

"There's a hope," Harry said, and she glared at them both as they went out the door.

Men. Always assuming they knew what was best, always stomping around, always—

She wanted Harry. The thought appeared from out of nowhere and totally screwed up her concentration. She was a rational adult woman, well past the age of making stupid mistakes involving sex. She was much too smart to get involved with anybody like Harry, especially since Harry seemed to loathe her because all he did was yell at her, but she didn't believe that, either.

Harry wanted her. She wanted Harry. Harry wasn't going to do anything about it. So that left her.

"Don't be stupid," she said out loud, and then wondered which would be stupider, trying to seduce Harry or deciding not to and spending the rest of her life wondering what would have happened if she'd had the guts to take the risk.

If you're not risking, you're not living, Janice had said.

The hell with it. "Here's to life," Victoria said, and picked up the phone to call room service.

As soon as Alec left, Dennie splashed cold water on her face to get her thoughts back where they belonged and reapplied her makeup. Bondman would care about stuff like makeup, and he was definitely her next stop. If Alec wasn't going to meet him until eleven, maybe he'd show up early in the bar and she could catch him, apologize, suggest they meet the next afternoon to talk. If she hadn't totally screwed up with the crack about Al Gore, he'd go for it. He'd been scoping her out ever since she got to the hotel; he'd definitely go for it.

The phone rang as she was heading out the door, and she stopped to get it in case it might be Alec. Not that Alec mattered.

It was Taylor.

"Dammit, I warned you, Banks," he yelled, and Dennie sat down hard on the bed.

"I didn't talk to her," Dennie said. "I haven't said a word."

"No, but you stared at her all the way through some speech this morning," Taylor said. "I told you—"

"You told me *after* that speech," Dennie said. "You're about a beat behind here. I sat in the back and I didn't say a word to anybody. I'm innocent."

"Stay away from her," Taylor said. "Because I do not enjoy getting these damn phone calls. One more, and you're fired, Banks, I mean it. I don't give a damn how good you are at weddings."

"Thank you, Taylor," Dennie said, and hung up.

If she went near Victoria tomorrow and Janice saw her, she was dead. She should call and cancel now. After all, she had the Bondman story.

Dennie looked at the phone as if it were a snake. If she called, she'd never get to hear Janice talk about risking and marriage and what it all meant. She'd never get to ask her the questions she'd found in Janice's writings. She'd never get to write the interview.

The smart thing to do would be to call Victoria and cancel.

The risky thing to do would be to have breakfast.

162

The clock clicked over a number, and Dennie saw she had only fifteen minutes to set up Bondman.

The hell with smart. She shoved the phone away and went to find her second story.

Bond sat in the bar and thought about the brunette and the dweeb professor he was about to meet. Why the hell a babe like that would prefer some teacher to him was a mystery, since she was obviously no dummy. She'd almost blown it for him, right there. Thank God the dweeb was clumsy.

He felt somebody slide into the seat beside him, somebody brunette, his peripheral vision told him before he turned, hoping for a split second that it was Dennie before he saw who it really was.

"Sherée?" He practically goggled at her, and she smiled, obviously pleased to have the upper hand.

"Thought you'd lost me forever, huh?" she said, and snuggled a little closer.

Oh, great. It wasn't that he didn't want her

around so much as he didn't want her around *now.* "Sherée, you've got to get out of here," he said, moving away a little. "I'm meeting a mark, and I don't want to have to explain you. He's ready to buy. Get lost, and I'll see you later."

"He," Sherée repeated with suspicion. "You're not after some other girl, are you?"

Bond closed his eyes. It had been a good ten years since anyone could have referred to Sherée as a girl, but she hadn't caught on yet. "It's a guy. Now get out of here. He's coming in anytime."

"What's your room number?" Sherée asked. "Give me the key. I'll wait up there."

Bond thought about saying no, but knowing where Sherée was had its advantages, not the least of which was that he wouldn't have to sleep alone that night. "814," he said, handing the card over. "I'll be there by one. Now get lost."

Sherée kissed his cheek and slid off the stool, and he watched in the mirror as she headed for the door. She stepped back to let another woman come through, and Bond clutched his drink tighter as he saw it was Dennie Banks.

Sherée kept going, and he relaxed again until

Dennie came and sat beside him. "Mr. Bondman?" she said, and he turned, intending to be cool and remote. That plan died a sudden death when he saw how close she was and how lovely she was.

"Miss Banks," he said, and she smiled regretfully and shook her head.

"Dennie, please," she said. "Alec has just been reading me the riot act about how I behaved at dinner so I wanted to slip down and apologize before you met him. He explained the Washington fix to me, and I see now how wrong I was."

Bond didn't want to believe her, but she looked so imploring, and she was so charming. . . .

"Sometimes I get a little protective of Alec and his aunt because they have so much money," Dennie went on. "And I am very attracted to Alec, although he's not really, well, smart." Her smile deepened, "I like clever men, but Alec has a lot going for him too."

Yeah, like a lot of money, Bond thought, and cheered up. If Dennie Banks was a gold digger, she'd be a lot easier to handle. "Alec could make a lot of money on this deal," he told her. "Double his investment easily."

Dennie leaned a little closer and licked her lips. *Greedy,* he thought. *Greedy with a great mouth. Things are going nicely.*

"Could I talk with you tomorrow afternoon?" she asked. "Maybe here in the bar? I'd really like to know all about this investment and the money."

"Certainly," he found himself saying.

"And, if it's all right with you, we just won't tell Alec about this," Dennie went on. "He's just a little jealous, you know?"

"Right." Bond glanced uneasily over his shoulder. If Prentice was jealous, he didn't want to get caught moving on something the dweeb was interested in. "Tomorrow."

Dennie smiled at him and slid off the stool. "Tomorrow," she said, and moved out of the bar, her sway hypnotic even beneath the severe black dress she was wearing.

Prentice showed up only minutes later, looking a little grim, and Bond had a moment of panic that he'd been seen with Dennie and the deal was off. Then Prentice smiled his usual dweeb smile, and Bond relaxed.

"Hey, thanks for meeting me," Prentice said,

offering Bond a limp handshake. What a wuss. Bond faked a hearty greeting.

"My pleasure, Alec. Sure hated to see you leave like that at dinner."

"Well, covered with wine, you know." Prentice fumbled with a coaster and knocked an ashtray off the bar. "Sorry."

Bond put the ashtray back. "No problem."

"Sorry about Dennie too," Prentice said. "Speaks before she thinks sometimes, but a good heart."

"Fine woman that Dennie," Bond said. "Glad you could tear yourself away to meet me."

"She sent you her best," Prentice said. "Said she jumps to conclusions sometimes. Sorry about all that." Bond nodded, and the bartender appeared. "Rum and Coke," Prentice said. "Oh, and make that a diet Coke, please."

"Make that two," Bond said, beaming. And then he thought, *Getting this guy's money and his woman will be a piece of cake.*

Upstairs in his room, Harry fumed over his third bourbon from the minibar. If anybody was going to put Vic in a condo, it was going to be him, not Donald—

No, he wasn't. He must be losing his mind. He was not going to put Vic in a condo. He wasn't going to put Vic anywhere.

Unbidden, images of where he could put Vic rose before him.

Oh, hell, he thought, *I should have stayed in Chicago.*

Alec called Harry at midnight, as soon as he was finished with Bond.

"It's sewed up," he said. "We're having dinner with Bond tomorrow night to celebrate the deal and that's when I'll sign the papers. We've got him."

"Wait till the checks come in tomorrow," Harry said. "We don't have him until we have him."

"You're right," Alec said. "You're always right. You were right about the Banks woman too. She was talking to him at the bar right before I got there. I had to duck out of the way or she'd have seen me. And they were pretty cozy considering she'd just been spitting at him at dinner."

"I'm sorry," Harry said, and the regret in his voice knocked Alec off stride.

"Thanks," he said, after a moment. "No offense, but that's not like you, Harry. Why aren't you gloating that you were right?"

"Sometimes being right is lousy," Harry said. "You okay?"

"Hey, she meant nothing to me," Alec said. "Get some sleep."

"Right," Harry said, as if that were the last thing in the world he'd be doing, and hung up.

"Harry?" Alec said, and then hung up, too, and stretched out on his bed. It was a lonely bed, and he remembered the one he'd been in a couple hours earlier with more regret than he'd thought possible.

So he'd lied to Harry. Dennie mattered. But she was a crook, so it was all just too bad.

Alec rolled over and put the pillow over his head and did his damnedest not to think about Dennie Banks.

Chapter 6

Harry had given up not thinking about Victoria. He'd been wrestling with his thoughts all night, trying to shove everything about her away, and it wasn't working. Even though he knew it was a dumb thing to do, he was going to have to go see her. Never a man to agonize over a foregone conclusion, Harry headed for the nineteenth floor.

Harry got to Victoria's door at the same time as room service. Room service was carrying a bottle of Champagne and two glasses.

"I'll take those," Harry said, and signed the check, tipping the waiter lavishly. Then he knocked on Victoria's door, trying to keep his heart from pounding through his chest.

When she opened the door, she was in her lace robe.

"I just took these away from room service," he said. "Who's the Champagne for? I'm warning you, if you've got Donald Compton in there, there's going to be blood on the carpet."

Victoria leaned on the door, looking better than any woman had a right to. "I ordered the Champagne," she told him, and there was a quiver in her voice. "I had plans to call you up here for a conference and seduce you, but now that you're yelling at me again—" Harry swallowed, stuck on the word "seduce," so Victoria kept going, her nervousness as plain as her exasperation. "Listen, you big galoot, I'm getting tired of opening and closing this door around you. If you come in here again, you're staying the night."

"Oh, yeah," Harry said, finding his voice at last. "And how are you going to stop me if I try to leave?"

Victoria untied her belt with one swift pull and shrugged the lace robe to the floor.

"That should do it," Harry said, and moved toward her, kicking the door shut behind him.

Alec spent the night staring at his ceiling, trying to dislike Dennie for being a crook and ending up trying to figure out ways to save her, instead. It was definitely time he got out of fieldwork permanently. He'd never thought about letting a bad guy get away before, but now all he could think about was getting her out of the picture before they arrested Bond. Well, not all he could think about. There were those eyes and those lips and that body and that laugh and the heat he'd seen in her eyes when he'd wrapped himself around her. *Think about the job,* he told himself, and then he thought about Dennie some more.

The thing about Dennie was that she was the kind of woman he could spend the rest of his life with and not get bored. He'd never tripped across that kind of woman before, and he had an idea they were few and far between so he'd better hold on to this one. If Harry was right, and she was a crook, he had less than forty-eight hours to convince her to change careers. Then he'd have to convince her to move to a strange city so they could get to know each other better. And along the way his hormones would appreciate it if he could talk her into bed too.

"No problem," he said out loud, and then rolled over and tried to go to sleep again.

Dennie spent the night staring at the ceiling, trying to figure out how she was going to survive if Taylor fired her, trying not to think about Alec but thinking of him obsessively anyway. *This is purely physical,* she told herself, and she knew she lied and wondered when Alec had become more than great kisses and juvenile banter over dinner. *Forget him, think of the stories,* she told herself, *think of Walter and his dog biscuits,* but she thought of him again anyway, and finally fell asleep in the thin light of dawn, thinking of his smile, and his hands, and his lovely long body, and how much she was going to miss him when he was gone.

* * *

Harry watched the dawn come up through Victoria's window as she nestled warm against him. When she started to stir, he kissed the top of her head where it rested against his chest.

"I've got to go, love," he whispered. "I don't want Bond to see me leaving your room." He thought for a moment. "Or Alec for that matter. He'd probably beat me up for seducing you."

Victoria laughed sleepily. "Who seduced who?"

He grinned into her curls. "I think we both did pretty good."

"I think we were both phenomenal." She held him tighter. "Don't go yet." She kissed him on the chest, laughing a little when he drew in his breath.

"Stop distracting me," he said. "You know, we have a decision to make here."

Victoria sighed, and moved back to her side of the bed. "Is this about Bond again?"

"No." Harry drew her back. "Pay attention. This is about us."

Victoria sat up. "Us?"

Harry looked at her with alarm. "Don't you think there's an us?"

"Of course I think there's an us." Victoria swallowed. "I just didn't think that you'd think there was an us."

Harry looked at her in outrage. "What do you think I am, nuts?"

"Yes," Victoria said, relaxing against his chest again. "But I'm crazy about you anyway."

Harry sighed, and tried again. "I live in Chicago. You live in Columbus. This is not going to work."

"We could see each other on weekends," Victoria offered. "It's only a forty-five-minute flight."

Harry scowled at her. "No, we couldn't. We have maybe twenty years left together. Less if you drive me crazy, and I kill you. We are not going to see each other on weekends."

"Could you get a transfer?" Victoria asked.

"The fraud department doesn't do a lot of work in Columbus," Harry said. "Cows don't do much investing."

"What cows?" Victoria asked, and then went on without stopping because she knew what was coming. "You want me to quit, don't you? You want me to give up my career. You want me to give up forty years of work."

"Well," Harry said, drawing away a little. "One of us is going to have to. If not you, me."

"You'd hate not working," Victoria said. "Alec says you'll never retire. I can't ask you to quit."

"One of us is going to have to," Harry said. "Which one?"

"Don't make me make that decision," Victoria said, close to tears. "That's not fair."

"Okay," Harry said. "I'll make it. You quit."

"Dammit, Harry." Victoria sat up, and this time Harry did too.

"Like I said, it's a decision." He rolled until his feet were on the floor and then he picked up his pants. "And it's probably one we shouldn't make naked. We can talk about this later."

Because you have work to do, Victoria thought. But all she said was, "You're right. Let me think about this."

When he was gone, she fell back into the bed and closed her eyes. If she quit her job, would she even know who she was? She'd just met Harry; it would be really stupid to throw away everything on the basis of a one-night stand with a man who had the personality of sandpaper. She thought of Harry, rasping his way through life, and smiled in spite of herself. Harry or her career.

Oh, hell, she thought, and buried her head under her pillow.

At roughly the same time, Sherée woke up and peered half asleep at Bond, who was completely asleep next to her. Thank God he slept like the dead. It was the only way she'd ever kept one step ahead of him. She slid quietly from the bed and picked up his jacket from the chair next to the desk. His appointment book was where it always was—inside front breast pocket—and she flipped through it, scouring the past two days. Appointments with the marks he'd told her about last night, the Compton guy and the Prentice woman. Both of them real old-timers, Brian had said, although he'd said the woman had probably been something once. Now she was half gaga, the perfect mark.

Sherée turned to the page for today, Saturday. Dinner with Compton and Prentice again to celebrate the deal, just as he'd said, but who was "Dennie, one, in bar"? He hadn't mentioned a Dennie. Sherée's eyes narrowed. One of Brian's many problems as a significant other was his interest in all women. If this Dennie was somebody he was chasing . . .

Brian stirred, and Sherée shoved the book in the jacket pocket and crawled back into bed. "What are you up so early for?" he muttered, trying to focus on her.

"I'm worried," Sherée said, stalling. "I can't sleep. What if we get caught?"

"I told you," he mumbled, rolling away from her, "we can't get caught. This time we're legal." He fell silent then, and in a few minutes he began to snore softly and Sherée relaxed.

He was doing something legal? Maybe he was going straight. Maybe everything would be all right, after all. The problem was, it just didn't sound like Brian. He was never legal or innocent or truthful. She thought about the appointment book again. One thing for sure, Sherée told herself as she punched her pillow and prepared to go back to sleep, she was going to check out Dennie in the bar at one. Compton and Prentice might be dupes, but she wasn't going to be.

At ten, Dennie headed for the Ivy Room a little light-headed from lack of sleep and more than a little nervous from what she was going to do. She'd rehearsed several different approaches to convince Victoria to help her with Janice, but when she sat down across from her, she took one look and forgot them all. Victoria's usual amiable smile was gone, and she looked troubled instead.

Dennie picked up the heavy red damask napkin by her plate. "What's wrong? You look upset."

Victoria blinked at her, as if she'd appeared out of nowhere. "Good morning, dear." She focused on her, and her smile came back. "No, I'm not upset. Just . . . puzzled. Things to work out." Her smile was full wattage now. "I ordered coffee and juice and a basket of muffins to start us out. Too hungry to wait."

"Works for me," Dennie said. "What are you puzzling? The Prentice compound?"

Victoria beamed at her. "Isn't it a wonderful idea?"

"No," Dennie said. "It stinks on ice. That man is a crook, and you are not dumb, which means you know he's a crook." Victoria looked slightly stunned so Dennie patted her hand. "I really want to know all about it, but I can wait on that. But I need to convince you to do me a huge favor, and I'm not sure how to go about it. What's a good way to convince you to do something?"

The waiter brought the drinks and muffins, and Dennie smiled around him at Victoria, exuding honesty and charm as fast and as hard as she could so Victoria would be bowled over by her openness.

"You're like Alec," Victoria said when the waiter had gone, and Dennie thought for a minute that she might be still doing her vague act. "He charms the socks off people, too, and then they wonder why they trusted him. It's because he does the fake openness so well. Everything about him says, 'Trust me on this,' and the whole time he has an agenda."

"I just said I had an agenda," Dennie protested.

Victoria picked up a muffin and split it with her knife. "Yes, but you said it with such charm, you knew I'd be disarmed." She buttered it calmly and then took a bite. "I'm not. You're up to something. What do you want?"

Dennie picked up a muffin to buy time. Blueberry, she noticed when she split it open. She hated blueberry. Bad omen. "I'm a reporter," she said. Might as well get the bad news over with first.

"That's a relief," Victoria said. "Until you insulted Brian Bond at the dinner table last night, we thought you were a thief." She polished off the first half of her muffin with a great deal of zest. "I'm fairly sure there are about three hundred fat grams in each of these. I plan on having at least one more."

"You thought I was a thief?" Dennie said. "You thought I was working with Bondman?"

Victoria poked through the muffin basket. "There must be another blueberry in here."

Dennie handed her plate over. "*Alec* thought I was a thief?"

"Thank you," Victoria said, taking the plate. "He hated it. I've never seen him more reluctant to arrest anybody."

"The son of a bitch," Dennie said conversationally. "At one point, I actually considered *sleeping* with him."

Victoria shoved the muffin basket at her. "Well, consider it again. He's very sweet, and he seems quite taken with you."

"You want me to sleep with somebody who's going to put me in jail?" Dennie shook her head. "I don't think so."

"I'll tell him not to now." Victoria polished off the last of her first muffin and started on Dennie's. "So you're a reporter. What does that have to do with me?"

Dennie shoved Alec aside for the moment and went back to Plan Z, the one Victoria had forced on her, honesty. "I want you to get me an interview with Janice Meredith," Dennie said, and Victoria said, "No," without missing a beat.

"See, this is why I do the charming bit," Dennie

said, exasperated. "When I stick to charming, people say yes. If I tell the truth, people say no."

Victoria frowned, obviously considering the situation, and Dennie went back to the muffin basket. Orange-coconut. Much better. She reached over and swiped Victoria's empty plate and began to butter.

"Why should I?" Victoria said. "She's my friend. She's going through a terrible time. Why should I turn you loose on her?"

"Because she's going to have to do an interview sooner or later," Dennie said, trying to be reasonable. Victoria should be able to figure this stuff out for herself. "And I'm on her side. I *admire* her. I'm changing my whole life because of what she said in the restaurant. I really do want to help her." Victoria looked unconvinced, so Dennie moved on to logic. "That fool Tallie Gamble will be talking to every rag in the country. All Janice needs to do is give one preemptive interview and she'll spike Tallie's guns good. If she'd talk to me right away, she could even be the one to announce the divorce. It just makes sense."

"Not to somebody who's supposed to be an

expert on marriage." Victoria stopped inhaling muffins and sipped her coffee, slower now, more thoughtful. "This is a large helping of crow, and you want her to serve it to herself?"

"She's an expert on relationships," Dennie said. "Sometimes those end. That's one of the things I wanted to talk to her about. I found this wonderful quote from Margaret Mead. Somebody asked her how she explained the failure of her marriages, and she said, 'What failure? I had three marriages and none of them were failures.' Think what Janice could do with that."

Victoria looked intrigued but not convinced so Dennie plowed on. "Besides, she's the one going around talking about risking and then hiding behind the cops. If she really believes in risking, I'm her best bet. I *believe* in her."

Victoria pushed her plate away. "What cops?"

"She's threatened to have me arrested for stalking," Dennie said. "That's why I needed Alec to get to you, and you to get to her. So I wouldn't be stalking her."

"So you were using Alec to get Janice, while

Alec was using you to get Bond." Victoria grinned. "I like that. It's tidy."

"Victoria, concentrate," Dennie said, and Victoria said, "Eat your muffin and listen to me."

Dennie sighed, and prepared to be patient while she chewed.

"Janice has built her entire career on understanding how marriage works." Victoria spoke carefully, as if she were arguing with herself, presenting points. "Charles isn't just leaving her for a younger woman, he's taking her career with him. Women like Janice and me have given up a great deal for our careers, and we don't regret it." She stopped, as if she were a little surprised. "I don't, you know. I fulfilled any maternal needs I had taking care of Alec and Andy in the summers. I don't regret one minute of my life."

Dennie nodded, still chewing, not sure how Victoria's summers had gotten into her interview, but too far in to back out now.

"But even without regrets, we aren't willing to see that kind of power taken away from us." Victoria straightened a little. "It's taken us forty years to get where we are today. That's something neither one of us is going to give up without a fight."

"Why?" Dennie said.

Victoria blinked at her. "Did you hear anything I said?"

"Everything." Dennie put the rest of her muffin down, the better to do battle. "Did you listen to yourself? You said the two of you have worked really hard to get where you are. Well, I know that. Everybody knows that. It's documented. You're published, people already know, you don't have to prove it anymore. In fact, proving it is redundant."

"That's not the point—" Victoria began, and Dennie cut her off.

"That's exactly the point. You've arrived. You've *done that*. What are you going to do now, just sit where you are and congratulate yourselves on having made the trip?" Dennie leaned closer, saying all the things to Victoria she meant to say later to Janice. "This is her chance to move on, to grow more instead of just resting where she is, digging herself in. She said it herself, if she's not risking, she's not growing."

Victoria swallowed. "Easy to say."

"I don't see that she has any choice, really." Dennie sat back. "She can try to pretend that nothing's changed and live the rest of her life blind and alone, or she can realize she's got a brand-new life ahead of her and embrace it no matter how rocky it is at first. And since she's a smart, tough woman who's come a long way in her life, I don't see her choosing to be blind for long. I wouldn't be surprised if she hadn't been feeling uneasy long before this."

"You're right," Victoria said, a faraway look in her eye. "I have been."

Dennie blinked and kept going, sweeping Victoria along with her. "Stephen Sondheim said, 'If you know where you're going, you've gone. Move on.' Seems to me Janice Meredith has known where she's been going for too long. I bet her husband sensed it. I bet he bailed before she could."

"What did you do, memorize *Bartlett's Familiar Quotations* before breakfast?" Victoria asked a little more tartly than the conversation called for.

"I've been researching for this interview like crazy," Dennie said. "I am prepared to get the greatest interview of all time. This is going to make my career, and it's not entirely selfish. This could be a great thing for Janice. This could make her not look like a loser, this could help her recover her balance. If she moves first, she's not the victim here, she's the smart one, the classy one. You know the psychologist Erich Fromm? He gave a lecture once, and a student held up his hand and said, 'But Professor Fromm, ten years ago you said A and now you're saying B.' And Fromm said, 'Are you sure I said A?' and the student nodded, and Fromm said, 'Well, I was wrong.' Isn't that the classiest thing you've ever heard? Don't you respect Fromm even more for coming out and saying it?" Dennie realized she was leaning over the table, almost flattening Victoria with her intensity, so she sat back. "I'm just giving Janice Meredith the chance to be a class act. She doesn't even have to say, 'I was wrong.' She just has to say, 'There's more to learn.' "

Victoria sat there frozen, and just when Dennie was going to ask if she was all right, she realized that Victoria's eyes were full of tears. Dennie sat dumbfounded for a moment before she moved to the chair beside her and handed her one of the damask napkins. "What did I say? I'm sorry."

Victoria took the napkin and dabbed at her eyes and then blew her nose on it. "You're right. You're absolutely right. Everything you said. There is more to learn. And I have known where I was going for too long. It's just really frightening, giving it all up and starting over."

"No kidding," Dennie said. "My job's on the line here, and I can't afford to lose it. But I can't stay where I've been either. That's why I need this interview."

"All right." Victoria gave one final sniff and shoved the napkin down next to her plate. "You're right. I'm seeing her this afternoon. I'll talk to her then."

Victoria stood, and Dennie felt a spurt of panic. "Listen, be careful, please. This woman is very serious about having me arrested."

"Janice would never do that," Victoria said.

"I think I may see a different side of her than you do," Dennie said. "And I'm fairly sure it's important to my career that I stay out of the slammer."

"Risking is everything," Victoria said, and headed for the door, and Dennie put her head down on the table and prayed that this was one risk that was going to pay off.

"I don't know what's holding up those checks I asked for," Alec told Harry an hour later in his room. "I already know what the one on Dennie is going to say, but I'd be a lot happier if I knew the status of that land Bond's selling."

"Do you ever get tired of this?" Harry said.

"Hell, yes," Alec said. "I was about finished on the road anyway when you grabbed me. Too damn many nights sitting alone in dumpy hotel rooms with a bottle of Jack Daniel's in one hand, trying to remember who I was pretending to be. I just miss—" He stopped in time, remembering that telling his boss he missed being in charge might be taken as a hint he wanted Harry's job. Which he did, but he didn't want to lose Harry either. Seven years to retirement, Harry said, but nobody believed he'd retire then. Oh, well. If he had to work for somebody, he'd pick Harry every time.

Evidently Harry hadn't noticed Alec's hesitation. "I've done this all my life," he said. "This is who I am."

Alec scowled at him. "It is not. You are not a computer bureaucrat, and you know it. What's gotten into you?"

Harry shrugged. "Nothing. Are you sure we're set for Bond?"

"No," Alec said. "I just told you. The last of the checks haven't come in. Are you all right?"

Harry scowled at him, "It's all this waiting around. I get too much time on my hands, and I start to think."

"Well, there's your problem," Alec said. "You're too old to start doing new things."

Harry snarled and stomped out of the room.

"That was a joke, Harry," Alec called after him, but Harry had already slammed the door.

By two-thirty that afternoon, Dennie was exhausted from a combination of no sleep the night before, worry about Victoria and Janice, and a steady loss of energy as she focused everything she had on Bond to convince him that she was really, really on his side after all. She'd explained her skepticism, offered her willingness to be convinced, listened to the story of his childhood, his dreams, his hopes, and slurped down two daiquiris in the hour and a half she'd been romancing the con. If nothing else, she'd have a great personal essay: "My Drunken Afternoon with a Land Shark."

"So, tell me more about your work." Dennie smiled shyly at him over the remains of her daiquiri. "It must be fascinating. Real estate, I mean."

Bond looked wary. Dennie's smile widened, and he looked less wary.

"Victoria is so excited about the investment, and you're so honest, I just have to give up all my skepticism. I think the Prentice compound is just a darling idea, and it's so clever of you to have thought of it." Dennie gazed admiringly at him through her lashes. "Tell me all about it."

Another daiquiri later, Dennie was ready to throw up, but she had her story, or at least a good start on it. She needed more information, but not this afternoon. She'd had all of Brian Bond, God's gift to women, that she could stomach, not to mention all of the daiquiris one woman could drink without barfing in a bar, and now she needed to brush her teeth, type her notes before she forgot them, and get some sleep before dinner with Alec the Rat.

"This has been so fascinating." Dennie slid off her stool, and her feet hit the ground with more impact than she'd been planning. Great. She'd had too much to drink. Time for a fast exit. "Maybe we could meet again. Tonight at dinner? I want to know everything about the Keys."

Bond's arm slid around her as he stood up. "How about tonight after dinner? Once Alec is in bed—"

"I'm sorry." Dennie tried to slide away. "Alec gets *so* jealous. I can't."

Evidently emboldened by his own daiquiris, Bond swooped down on her and kissed her, sliding his tongue in her mouth before she could clamp her lips shut.

His tongue reminded her of a raw oyster, but

she managed not to gag, staying with the kiss while thinking about how much she wanted this story. This was her backup if Janice Meredith failed her. A woman couldn't have too many stories. *Think of the stories.*

When he and his tongue called it quits so he could breathe, she stepped back.

"Brian, you animal," she said, and shook her finger at him, trying hard not to spit. "I can't trust you at all."

He smiled back, debonairly, and she felt like gagging again. No wonder she'd never gone for the tough interviews before. You had to have a stomach of steel to get them. She backed away, wiggling her fingers playfully at him, and then staggered out the door.

Alec was in the lobby, his arms folded in front of him, looking really unhappy with her.

This was the rat who had planned to arrest her even while he was kissing her on her own bed. No-good rat.

He looked really good for a no-good rat.

Dennie walked toward him, trying very carefully not to be unsteady. "Stop looking at me like that," she told him when she reached him. "I know he's awful. I'm just trying to find out about this swamp he's trying to sell you. Although you're such a rat, I should let him sell it to you."

Alec perked up a little and took her arm to steady her. "You have no taste in men," he said. "Also you're drunk."

"Right both times," she said. "I think I'll go back to my room and pass out."

"I'll come with you," he said. "You need somebody to chaperone you back to your room in case you decide to pick up a bellboy."

"And the chaperone is you?" Dennie shook her head. "I don't think so."

"You don't think at all." Alec steered her to the elevator bank and punched the button for her floor. "I can't believe you actually touched that guy with your mouth." He looked at her as if waiting for a reaction, and she stuck her tongue out at him. "You got any mouthwash?" he said.

"He has a tongue like a raw oyster." Dennie's mouth scrunched up at the memory.

The elevator doors opened, and Alec gave her a gentle shove. "That I did not need to know."

"You can't imagine how awful it was."

"I don't want to imagine. Could we change the subject?"

The elevator doors had closed, and they were leaning against the red velvet back wall when Dennie realized that she had only half the story, the Bond half. To get the whole nine yards, she needed Alec's side too. She looked at him out of the corner of her eye. He looked relaxed. What the hell. After all, her technique had worked beautifully on Bond. She turned her head and looked deep into Alec's eyes. "At least Bond told me what he does for a living. You've never done that. What do I have to do to get that out of you?"

"Oh, yeah, he told you what he does—" Alec began, and then she stretched up and kissed him.

Her neck felt boneless, partly because of the multiple daiquiris and partly because kissing Alec always made her feel boneless. And since kissing him was at the moment a professional obligation, she put her back into it, arching and sliding against him with a liquid grace that made him first clutch at her, and then slide his hands down to her rear and pull her close to him while his tongue stroked her mouth and she drowned in his kiss.

"God, you kiss beautifully," she said, moments later, trying to remember why she was playing with fire. "Is that what you do for a living? Kiss?"

"No," Alec said, dazed. "Although I'm considering it now. This is great." He bent his head to her again, and she ducked gracefully away.

"So what *do* you do?" she asked, struggling to get her breathing under control.

"I—" Alec began, and then stopped, a grin breaking slowly across his face. "Please, God, let this be happening. Don't let it be a lie."

"What?"

Alec cast a fervent gaze at the elevator ceiling. "Please let her be trying to seduce information out of me. Please let it be true."

"Oh, very funny." The elevator doors opened at the seventh floor, and Dennie walked out carefully.

"Wait, don't give up." Alec followed her out. "You can do it. Kiss me again."

"Drop dead." Dennie fished in her purse for her room card and jammed it in her door. Then she stepped inside, trying to shut the door in Alec's face, but he slipped in behind her while she was turning around.

She had to give up daiquiris as part of her investigative technique. They made her slow. And evidently stupid. Trying to seduce Alec for information was definitely stupid. Trying to seduce Alec at all was a waste of time; he came preseduced anyway. Like a microwave entrée. You pressed his buttons, and he got hot.

Well, she had work to do. And great kissers were . . . well, not a dime a dozen. But not on her agenda.

Right. She had an agenda.

"Leave," she said, but Alec was already stretched out on her bed and reaching for the phone.

"You need carbohydrate to soak up that alcohol," he told her. "Go rinse your mouth out while I order. I can't believe you kissed me with the same mouth that kissed him. Save me some mouthwash."

Dennie put her hands on her hips and glared. "You don't need to worry. It won't happen again."

"Want to bet?" He grinned at her. "You still haven't wormed any secrets out of me."

"You need worming all right," Dennie said. "You're about ninety-five percent worm. I want a steak. Very—"

"Rare. I know. I know everything you like."

Dennie winced. "God, you even sound like him."

"Like who? Bond? I do not." Then room service answered, and Alec turned his attention to the phone.

"Just like him," Dennie said, and went to wash out her mouth.

Downstairs in the lobby, Sherée fumed. Right, just a mark, that's all this Dennie person was. Then why was he all over the woman like that? She'd been right not to trust him with another woman.

Now all she had to do was get even.

"Okay, you're fed and at least relatively sober," Alec said an hour later. "Let's get back to the seducing part."

"In your dreams," Dennie said.

He was still stretched out on her bed, but she was sitting cross-legged at the foot, a whole bed length away from him.

"I can't believe you thought that would work," Alec said.

"It worked on Bond," Dennie said. "Come on, Alec, give. He's selling land. You're not dumb enough to be buying from him. So you're investigating him. What are you? SEC? FBI?"

"Don't be ridiculous." Alec grinned at her. The more she trashed Bond, the happier he got. Men were so transparent when they were jealous. Alec went on, "Do I strike you as somebody who'd work for an acronym?"

"Then who do you work for?"

He crooked a finger at her. "Oh, no. You have to seduce it out of me. Come here."

"You're some kind of cop," Dennie said, staying put. "It's the only thing that makes sense. I bet Bond would know. Maybe I'll ask."

Alec stopped, and then slowly sat up on the bed until he was close to her. He reached for her neck and encircled it with one firm hand. "Do not mention this fantasy to Bond."

"Or what?" Dennie said, unfazed. "You'll wring my neck? Ha."

"Ha, yourself," Alec said, and kissed her, pulling his hand down her neck and across her breast, his thumb tracing a pattern down the hollow of her throat and into her dress.

It felt great, but she was too close to the truth to stop now. Dennie caught his hand as it cupped her breast. "Who do you work for?"

"Harry Chase," Alec said. "I'll introduce you tomorrow. He's busy right now. And so are you." He dipped his head to kiss her again, and she slid away.

"And who does Harry Chase work for?"

Alec slid after her, rolling her under him and trapping her on the bed. "The KGB. We're Russian spies. This is your chance to be a patriot. Seduce me witless, and I'll tell you all my secrets."

"Are you a crook?" Dennie asked. Her hands were firm against his chest, and she wasn't playing. "If you're a crook like that slime Bond, I'm not interested."

"Do you think I'm a crook?" He smiled his open, honest boyish smile at her.

"I think you could be." Dennie stared back, unsmiling. "I think you'd probably do just about anything if you thought the reason was right. And I haven't known you long enough to know what reasons you think are right."

Alec stared down at her, suddenly serious. "I'm not a crook. I'm one of the good guys. But you're just going to have to take my word for that. Which is only fair because that's what I'm doing for you right now, much against my better judgment."

Dennie felt her breath go, and not just because of all of Alec's lovely weight on top of her. "This is the first time I've seen you serious," she said. "This is really you, isn't it?"

Alec's face changed, and it felt as if he'd moved closer, although that wasn't physically possible. "Yes," he whispered, and kissed her, and this time Dennie felt more than the old, hot physical punch of his kiss. This one hurt deep inside, breaking into a place she'd kept safe before, and she closed her eyes and held him tight and savored the pain because it was so agonizingly wonderful

to feel that much about anything, and especially
wonderful to feel that much about Alec. *I love
you,* she thought, but she didn't say it, saying it
would have been stupid. She'd known him only
forty-eight hours. She absolutely was not going to
tell Alec "I love you."

Alec must have heard her anyway. He broke
the kiss and closed his eyes as if he were as thrown
by it as she was. Then he rolled off her to sit on the
edge of the bed. "Listen, I'm not a crook. But I
very much need you not to blow my cover to
Bond."

Dennie sat up and tried to remember what they
were talking about. "I won't. I need to see Bond
again, though. I'm working on a story about him."

Alec frowned at her, pulling away even more.
"I thought you were working on Janice Meredith."

"I can do two things at once." Dennie held out
her hand. "But I won't get in your way, and I
won't blow your cover. Deal?"

Alec took her hand and held it. "No deal." He
started to say something and then he stopped,
leaning forward to kiss her on the cheek instead.
He hesitated as if he was going to move to her

mouth, and she held her breath, but then he stood up. "This thing with Bond is just about over, and it would have made a lousy story anyway, so do me a favor and forget him." Dennie started to shake her head but he went on. "You don't need to be there tonight, and I probably won't see you again before I go tomorrow. Have a good life, Dennie Banks. I'll watch for your byline in all the major publications."

He turned and left before she could think of what to say, and Dennie felt the bottom of her stomach plummet as the door closed behind him. It was probably all those damn daiquiris. So he was leaving. Big deal. There were other great kissers in the world. But if he thought she was giving up the Bond story, he was nuts.

Dennie let herself slip back down into the bed. Now she could concentrate on the two greatest stories of her career. She'd certainly handled everything beautifully. Patience would be so proud. She got her laptop and began her Bond notes. It was going to be a great story. She'd really handled things well.

Of course, Lady Macbeth had probably felt the same way after she'd washed off all that blood.

Stupid analogy. Dennie hadn't killed anybody. She didn't have anything to regret.

With a great deal of willpower, Dennie dragged her mind back to her story and began to type but it was no go. *You just need sleep,* she told herself, and slid down into her bed and stuck her head under the pillow and tried her damnedest not to think about Alec.

When Alec got back to his room, he found a message from Harry telling him to meet them in Harry's room. *Why?* Alec thought. What difference did any of this make? They'd put Bond away for a little while, and then he'd be out on parole, and the whole mess would start over again in another state. Even Harry's database couldn't stop these guys; it would just make them easier to catch.

And that was something, Alec had to admit. It just wasn't everything anymore. He shoved that thought aside and went to tell Harry that he was pretty sure Dennie wasn't a con.

* * *

"I know," Harry said, when Alec was in his room. Harry sat on the edge of the brass-bound desk by the window and looked despondent. Victoria sat in the red plush desk chair and looked worse. Harry went on. "The checks came back. She's a reporter, nothing to do with Bond."

"I told you so," Victoria said, but she didn't look happy.

Neither did Harry. Well, Alec didn't feel particularly joyful either. They weren't supposed to be happy. They were working.

"I told her not to bother about tonight," Alec said. "She wanted to do a story on the whole mess. I just want it over with."

"So do I," Harry said. "But we hit a snag. A big one."

"A snag?" Alec looked at them both warily. "I do not want to hear about snags."

"Well, you're going to—" Harry snapped, and then Victoria cut him off.

"The two of you seem to have missed a detail," Victoria said acidly. "Evidently, it is not illegal to sell land you own."

* * *

When the phone rang half an hour into her nap that afternoon, Dennie stretched out a hand from under the covers to pick it up, more to stop it from ringing than from any desire to talk to anyone. She had to pat the table twice before she found the phone, and even then she dropped the receiver on the bed before she managed to mumble, "H'lo?"

"Banks?"

Dennie frowned, trying to open her eyes. "What?"

"Banks?"

"Taylor?" She fumbled with the covers, trying to sit up and pull her thoughts together. "Taylor, is that you?"

"It certainly is me." The satisfaction in Taylor's voice was clear, even through her stupor.

"Taylor, what do you want?" Dennie looked longingly at the soft place she'd been in bed. "I'm busy here."

"Not anymore you're not," Taylor said. "You're fired."

Chapter 7

Back in Harry's room, Alec closed his eyes in pain. "He owns the land?"

"Yeah," Harry said. "It's crap, nobody will ever be able to develop it, but he can sell it. He owns it."

"Oh, hell." Alec sat down and put his head in his hands so he could think unimpeded by the relentless gloom in front of him. "Did he misrepresent anything?"

"No." Victoria seemed near tears. "He was everything he said he was. He never pretended to be anything else."

Harry reddened a little. "That EPA stuff wasn't a promise. We can't get him."

Alec looked from Harry to Victoria and back again. "Do you guys know something I don't? Because you look way too depressed for this. We'll figure this out."

"How?" Victoria slumped back in her chair. "Harry and I already talked about it. We agreed to the land deal as it stood. If we start asking him to make promises now, he'll smell a rat. We all sat there and agreed with him."

"Dennie didn't," Alec said. He'd meant it as a rueful joke, but as soon as he said it, he realized what it meant. "Dennie didn't go for the deal at all," he said, as he straightened. "If the deal hinged on Dennie, he'd have to pony up more."

Harry stopped looking at Victoria as if he were a basset hound and brightened. "This could be good."

"Of course, I just said good-bye to her forever," Alec said.

"Well, *that* was dumb," Victoria said tartly. "Of course, this is my day for dumb people. First Janice Meredith, the smartest woman I know, turns out to be a paranoid rabbit, and then there's you two. You meet the perfect woman and you sacrifice her for your job." She stood up and slammed her chair under the desk. "Men have absolutely *no* sense of priorities." ·

She stomped out of the room, and Harry said, "Oh, hell," and pulled her chair out and sat down.

"I'm missing a lot here," Alec said.

"Solve your own problems," Harry said. "What the hell did you dump Dennie for, anyway? You didn't know she wasn't a con. You should have played her." Harry's scowl deepened. "That's what you get for being unprofessional. The job always comes first."

"You can't dump somebody you never had," Alec said. "And if it turned out she wasn't a con— which I would like to point out, it did—we didn't need a reporter on this, we have enough trouble. And she was unpredictable."

"Unpredictable is bad," Harry growled in agreement.

Also she was screwing up my thinking to the point where I might have said something stupid, Alec went on silently. *Like, "I love you."* That would have been bad. You do not tell a woman you have known for forty-eight hours that you love her. Well, more like fifty hours because it had been noon on Thursday when she'd come smacking through the doors—

He stopped. Counting the hours since he'd met somebody was a bad sign.

"But we still need her," Harry said, finishing his sentence. "Go get her."

Alec grinned. He hadn't meant to, going back to Dennie was such a bad idea, but as soon as Harry said it, he felt better.

"Only because it's the professional thing to do," he told Harry, and went back to his room to figure out what to say when he called her.

Back in her room, Dennie clenched her jaw and told herself not to panic. "Taylor, I'm tired. Call back later with the jokes."

"Banks, you're fired." She heard no sympathy whatsoever in his voice. "I warned you about that Meredith woman, but you wouldn't listen."

Victoria. Dennie ran her hand through her hair

as she tried to make sense of what he was saying. Could Victoria have talked to Janice already? "Taylor, don't be ridiculous," she said, stalling for time so she could think. "I didn't go anywhere near her."

"Well, you went near somebody because she called the owner mad as hell this morning to say you'd been having dinner with somebody you shouldn't have, and he called me mad as hell, and you're fired."

Dinner. That meant it wasn't Victoria Janice was mad about. She really wanted her fired. The matter-of-fact satisfaction in Taylor's voice made Dennie go cold suddenly. "You're not kidding."

"Nope. You get two weeks' severance pay, and, Banks? I wouldn't ask for a reference."

"Taylor, c'mon now—"

"You asked for it, Banks. I warned—"

Dennie slammed the phone down before he could finish and then sat there, desperately trying to order her thoughts.

Fired. She really was fired. No job. No paycheck. No biscuits for Walter. Nothing. Two weeks' severance pay and then what?

And all just because she'd had dinner with Alec and his aunt?

She was beginning to dislike Janice Meredith.

The phone rang again, and she picked it up. "Listen, Taylor," she said, trying to keep the fear out of her voice.

"Who's Taylor?" Alec asked.

"I don't have time for you," Dennie said, overwhelmingly glad to hear from him, and overwhelmingly angry she was so glad. "You said good-bye, you rat. You made the big exit. Go away."

"Ten minutes. That's all I ask."

"Alec, I have *problems*. Go away!" Right before Dennie slammed the receiver down, she heard Alec say, "Don't hang up!" which made slamming it that much more satisfying.

Alec dialed again, taking the phone with him as he crossed his hotel room to stare out the window.

"That was childish," he said, when she picked it up the second time.

Her voice came across the wire, taut with

emotion. "I'm having a bad day. *Do not* tell me what to do."

Alec grinned. "All right then, I'm asking you, pleading with you. On bended knee. Groveling." He sat on the edge of the windowsill. "I swear to God, I'm wallowing on the carpet right now. My eyeballs are full of broadloom."

· "That's not all you're full of." The break in Dennie's voice was even rougher than usual. "I'm not kidding about a bad day. What do you want?"

Alec kept his voice light. "I need your help, Dennie. You and me, together again."

"No. You thought I was a crook, and then you dumped me because I was a reporter. The hell with you. I have to go."

"Look, I'm sorry I didn't trust you. I will apologize over and over if you meet me. I'll be happy to come to your room. Hot fudge sundaes on me." The silence on the other end wasn't encouraging so he got serious. "Dennie, this is important. You can help me get this guy."

"You want me to help you do your job?"

"Yes."

"What's in it for me?"

"What?" Alec's voice cracked in outrage.

Dennie's voice stayed sharp. "What's in it for me? Come on, Alec, you're getting paid for this. Would you do this if there was no paycheck involved?"

"Yes," Alec said, without hesitation. He stopped, surprised at himself. "Yes, I would."

"You would?" Dennie sounded as surprised as he felt, and suspicious too. "Why?"

"Let me come see you, and I'll tell you," Alec said.

"Here?" There was a long pause, and then her voice came back, grimly serious. "You swear you'll come clean? No tricks, no lies, no evasions?"

"Not about Bond," Alec said. "I reserve the right to revert to my usual devious self in other matters."

"There are no other matters between us," Dennie said.

"Well, we can talk about that too," Alec said. "I can be in your room in five minutes. What do you say?"

Alec waited out a long pause before she said,

"Come up. I will give you only fifteen minutes to explain, no hands, so you'd better talk fast."

"It's what I do best," Alec said.

"That's what I figured," Dennie said.

"Hey," Alec said, but she'd already hung up.

"You know, if you were serious about trying to win me over, you'd have picked something a little snazzier than room service hot fudge," Dennie told him half an hour later.

Alec was puzzled by the lack of lilt in her voice, but he was willing to play along. "Ah, but because of my keen sense of character, I could tell you were the deep intellectual kind of woman who wouldn't be swayed by fancy restaurants with fancy prices." He picked up the desserts from the room service tray, sat down on the bed next to her, and handed her a sundae.

"You were wrong." Dennie stabbed her spoon through the whipped cream to the fudge. "I am easily swayed by fancy restaurants. Also by diamonds and gold. Particularly by diamonds and gold. Particularly today."

She licked the fudge off her spoon, and Alec tightened beside her and then forced himself to relax. "So what happened this morning?" Alec slurped his own fudge and whipped cream.

"I got fired." Dennie put her sundae on the table beside her, evidently not hungry after all. She wrapped her arms around herself and stared at the blank TV.

Alec stopped slurping. "Fired?"

"My boss warned me to stay away from Janice Meredith," Dennie said, still staring at the TV. "So I did. Sort of. But for some reason, she had me fired anyway. My best guess was your aunt Victoria but Janice was mad before that."

"Aunt Vic wouldn't have you fired."

"No," Dennie said. "But she was going to talk to Janice for me this afternoon, and Janice might have decided that I was still harassing her. She decided something because she called the owner of the paper this morning." She turned her head to look at Alec. "And that's the end of my job."

Alec slid closer and put his free arm around her, balancing his top-heavy sundae in the other hand. "So we'll fix it."

"No," Dennie said. "I don't think this one is going to fix. I don't think I'm bouncing back from this one. In fact, I think I may even deserve this."

"Hey." Alec tightened his grip on her shoulders. "You don't—"

"I'm thirty-four," Dennie said. "It's time I tried the hard stuff. That's what this is, the hard stuff. This is the kind of experience that will make me smarter. I don't want to bounce back the same. This is my chance to grow up. To be tough."

"I like you soft," Alec said, puzzled. "And I've never noticed you being particularly weak or afraid, and you're sure as hell not a quitter—"

"I always have been." Dennie stared at the TV again. "Afraid, I mean. You know, my best friend and I used to spend the first two weeks of every summer at her uncle's farm. He had this big pond, almost a lake, and one side of it had this ledge hanging over it. It wasn't much of a ledge, maybe ten, fifteen feet, but to a kid, it was high."

"Okay," Alec said, trying to follow her drift.

"Every summer, Patience would just plunge off that cliff, and I'd be too afraid until she'd say, 'I'll catch you. Jump, I'll catch you.' And she always did. And now I'm really going to jump, and she's not going to be there." She squinted at Alec. "That's the only hard part. The rest of this, losing the job? That's not so tough, really. I needed to leave that job anyway. So it's scary, but good scary. It's knowing Patience can't catch me anymore because she's got a husband to catch now. She can't drop everything for me. I wouldn't ask her to. I'm going to have to do the tough stuff alone."

"No." Alec paused, trying to think of the right thing to say. "You're not alone." Alec moved his hand from her shoulder to drape his arm around her neck, hauling her closer to him, his chin against her hair. "I can cover you until you're ninety-six."

"Ninety-six." Dennie's voice sounded flat, and Alec felt a clutch of fear; maybe she wasn't going to come back from this one. After a moment, she pulled back from him and asked in the same flat voice, "Why ninety-six?"

Alec tilted her chin up until she was eye-to-eye with him. "Because when you're ninety-six, I'll be a hundred, and I'll be too damn old to break your fall. Until then, I've got you covered."

She swallowed, and the movement of her throat made him dizzy. He reached across her to put his sundae on the table and free up his hand for better things, and the melting cream slipped a little, a dollop falling right below Dennie's collarbone. "Sorry," he said, and bent to lick it from her skin. When he lifted his head again, her eyes didn't look dead anymore, and Alec felt his heart pound. *Careful,* he told himself, and then thought, *Screw careful.*

"Right," Dennie said, a little breathlessly. "You're planning on staying around until I'm ninety-six."

"No," Alec said, pulling her closer. "I am not planning on it. Hauling you out of trouble is the last thing a sane man would plan on. But I'll be there just the same."

Dennie seemed strangely calm. "You think?"

Alec took a deep breath. "I know. What do you think?"

"Oh, boy." Dennie smiled up at him, a weak

smile but a real one. "I don't know what I think, but I know it feels awfully good to hear you say it."

Alec traced her lips with his finger. "Well, that's a start. The important thing is, you know you're not alone in this." On an impulse, he kissed her forehead, and then her nose, and then gravity took him to her lips, and the kiss there was soft and light and comforting and made him breathless. "You're not alone, babe," he whispered against her lips, and then she buried her face against his neck, and he wrapped his arms around her and held her tightly.

When she pulled back a few minutes later, her face was flushed, but she was Dennie again. "You really know how to get to a woman, Prentice," she told him.

"It's my charm," he said. "Although you seem to be pretty resistant to it in general."

"My defenses are down this afternoon." Dennie snuggled closer. "God, you feel good."

"Remember that," Alec said, hating what he had to say next. "Because I have to change the subject here." She looked up at him then, and Alec said, "I need your help to get Bond." When she didn't say anything, he went on. "Brian Bond is a real estate con. He regularly swindles people out of their savings. He's bad, and he should be in jail, and my boss and I would like to put him there. But we need your help."

"I thought you had that under control," Dennie said, pulling away a little and frowning. "Didn't Victoria—?"

"We hit a snag. Bond owns the land he's selling."

Dennie's frown deepened. "So where's the fraud?"

"He's telling people it can be developed, and he's selling it for about ten times what it's worth."

"Oh, yeah." Dennie nodded. "The I've-got-the-EPA-fixed bit."

Alec shook his head. "He doesn't even tell them that. He says the EPA will be fixed, not specifically by him. He puts nothing on paper. He's not breaking the law." He scowled. "Except morally. By the time the people who have bought the land have caught on, he'll be long gone. And even if they caught him, they probably wouldn't have much recourse. They'll have paid prime dollar for worthless swamp, but as long as he didn't promise them anything different—"

Dennie broke in. "So where do I come in?"

"One of the selling points he's been using on me is what a great place this would be for me to settle down. And he's seen us together. As a matter of fact"— he paused, unsure of how she'd take the next part—"when I thought you were working with him, I told him you were the perfect woman. He thinks I'm crazy about you."

Dennie nodded, and her curls brushed his cheek and derailed his train of thought again. "I am the perfect woman," she said, "and you should be crazy about me. Get to the point."

I am crazy about you, Alec told her silently and then jerked his mind back to the problem at hand. "We get engaged, we meet Bond for drinks, I get ready to buy the property for you, and you spoil the deal."

Dennie blinked. "I what?"

Alec grinned. "You bat your eyes and tell me that you want a house, not a lousy piece of swamp. I tell Bond, no sale."

Dennie nodded. "I get it. And then he promises

us a house, which he can't deliver." She looked thoughtful. "Is he that dumb?"

"It won't be the first time he's sold something he didn't have," Alec said.

Dennie thought about it some more. "I'll do it. On one condition."

"Oh, hell," Alec said, letting go of her. "Can't you just do it out of the goodness of your heart?"

"No." Dennie folded her arms and set her chin. "I want the story."

"What story?"

"I want to break the story of the arrest. I want you to tell me everything you know about this guy, and I want to write the story. In depth."

"No," Alec said. "We have to take him to court. I can't—"

"No problem," Dennie said. "This isn't a newspaper story. I got fired, remember? This is a magazine article. An in-depth article I can peddle as a freelancer. It won't see print until after the trial. You can tell me all about how you work. It'll be great."

"My boss would never go for it," Alec said.

"Let me talk to him," Dennie said. "I'm good with men."

"Not with Harry." Alec shook his head. "Harry doesn't like women."

"Harry never met me."

"No."

"Then I won't do it." Dennie picked up her sundae and ate while Alec glared at her.

"I can't believe I was comforting you a minute ago, and now you're turning on me," he said, trying to sound indignant.

"Forget the guilt trip." Dennie grinned at him. "You can give me this story. You know you can."

"It'll blow my cover."

"I'll refer to you as a generic geek. Only those people who know you will recognize you from that description."

"Dennie—"

"I get the story, or you don't get me." Dennie spread her hands, one full of sundae, the other with the spoon, the picture of rationality. "I don't see the problem."

There was still a shadow behind the bravado, but she was Dennie again, and that threw him the way it always did. "How much of you do I get?" Alec asked.

"Probably not that much. So do we meet for dinner tonight?"

Alec gave up. "Yes."

"Thank you." Dennie smiled at him and dipped into her sundae again. "You won't regret this."

"I regret it already," Alec said. "We need to meet with Harry and Victoria this evening before we meet Bond. Is seven all right for you?"

"Why Victoria?" Dennie said.

"Victoria's going to sweeten the deal. She's going to dinner with us, and when she hears you talk about a house, she'll decide she wants one next door." Alec stopped, distracted for a moment by the beauty of the plan. "All that money, just lying there, and all he has to do to get it is lie. He'll do it." He narrowed his eyes, thinking about Bond.

"You really want him, don't you?" Dennie said.

"Yes." He met her eyes, deadly serious. "This is important. This guy should not be preying on people. He wipes out their savings and leaves them nothing, Dennie. Nothing. We've got to stop him."

Dennie blinked. "This is what you meant, isn't it? When you said you'd do it even if they didn't pay you. Because you're trying to save people."

"Hey, look, I'm not Robin Hood," Alec said, taken aback. "Don't make me into a hero. I do this for a living. It's a job."

"I bet the pay's lousy," Dennie said.

"It could be better," Alec said. "But look at the fun I have."

"I bet you could make a bundle doing something else."

Alec studied her, trying to see why she was suddenly so interested. "Probably," he said cautiously.

Dennie smiled at him. "You are really something else, Alec Prentice." She put her sundae on the table and then leaned over and kissed him on the cheek. "I don't know what you are exactly, but I like it, whatever it is, and I will be your baby tonight. No tricks. I promise."

She was so close that he couldn't resist. He turned his head and kissed her softly, and she put her hands on his chest and leaned into him, moving her lips against his until his arms went around her. She tasted of chocolate and of Dennie and of love, and he eased her down beneath him, losing himself in the way she moved into him.

"You love me," he whispered in her ear.

"Maybe," she whispered back, but she held him tighter and that was the better answer. "I love the way you feel against me, but I need to think about all of this, about who I am and what I want. I'm not making any more dumb moves."

"I am not a dumb move," Alec said, and he kissed her again, once, with all the passion he had for her, and when he broke the kiss and she blinked up at him, dazed, he said, "Think about that first, please," and then left her, still blinking at him.

It wasn't easy leaving her, he thought as her door closed behind him, but he was going to see her again that night. And if he had anything to do with it, a lot of nights after that.

Surprisingly cheered by the thought of commitment, Alec whistled all the way back to his room.

Harry knocked on Victoria's door at five-thirty with roses and Champagne, and when Victoria answered the door and saw it was him, she said, "I'm sorry I was so bitchy" and pulled him into her arms; he dropped the flowers and the Champagne and just held her until she pulled him toward the bed.

An hour later, Harry cuddled Victoria a little closer and said, "I was going to tell you something important when you jumped me at the door and then I forgot how to talk."

"I think you should stop bringing Champagne," she said into his chest. "We never drink it."

"Will you listen to me?" he said, tipping her chin up so he could look in her eyes, but she interrupted him.

"I called the university and resigned this afternoon," she said. "It took me all afternoon but I finally found the head of my department, and I resigned. I'm not even going back for next quarter."

"You what?"

"I resigned," Victoria said. "I bitched at you about your lousy priorities, and I knew the whole time mine were just as bad. So I picked love instead of work, and it's okay. I've always wanted to write, and now I can live with you and write, and we can make love every night. I can't think why I didn't jump at the chance the first time you mentioned it. This is going to be wonderful."

Her voice was relentlessly cheery, but he could hear the loss beneath the cheer. "It was tough, wasn't it?"

Victoria buried her face in his chest. "Yes," she said. "It was very tough. I've been teaching for forty years. And now I won't be." She pulled back her head to look at him. "Thank you for knowing that it was tough."

He kissed her gently. "I know because it was tough for me too."

Victoria froze in his arms. "What?"

"I called Chicago and resigned. Hardest thing I've ever done." He put his cheek against her hair.

"You resigned?"

"I recommended Alec for my job."

"Oh." Victoria held him tighter.

Harry tried to sound cheerful too. "Maybe I'll . write my memoirs. I'll tell you about all the brave things I've done, and you can be impressed and write them down."

Victoria was quiet for a moment, and then she said, "You did the bravest thing this afternoon. I'll be impressed about that forever."

They clung to each other, absorbing their losses and comforting themselves.

"You realize we can live anywhere now," Harry said after a while. "Anywhere at all."

"I can get us a great deal on some land in Florida," Victoria said, and they both started to laugh.

By the time dinner was over, nobody was laughing, and the only comfort Alec could take from the whole night was that at least he'd spent it with Dennie. She'd worn the red dress again, too, and every now and then he'd caught a flash of purple lace at the edge of her neckline. He'd been planning on catching more than a flash later, but that later was now, and they were still working.

Bond hadn't been as greedy as they'd hoped he'd be.

"I can't believe how slippery that little toad is," Victoria said when they were all back in her room.

"Where'd we go wrong, Harry?" Alec asked him. "I was there and I couldn't tell, but I might have been distracted. Did we say something that tipped him off?"

"If you did, I didn't hear it." Harry sat on the edge of the bed looking tired, and Alec thought that for the first time, the man looked his age. "You were all good. I don't know what happened. Maybe he's just a lot smarter than we figured."

Victoria went over and sat beside him. That was Aunt Vic, always comforting people, even people she didn't like. Alec felt a wave of gratitude toward her.

"I thought for sure when Donald agreed about the house that was it," she said. "Donald is so clueless that Bond has to believe him. He couldn't have turned us down because he didn't believe us. It must just be caution."

"He wanted to do it," Dennie said, and they all turned to look at her, surprised because they weren't used to hearing a fourth voice in their meetings. "Well, he did," Dennie said defensively. "You could see he wanted it. All that money. There were just too many of us."

Alec considered it. "She might have a point," he said finally.

"Might?" Dennie said. "Thank you very much."

Alec ignored her and went on. "All of us talking at once would put Bond on his guard whether he suspected anything or not. He'd have to be careful dealing with that many people. But if only one of us went down and talked to him, it could be different."

"Hell, it's worth a shot," Harry said.

Alec stood up. "I'll call him."

"No," Dennie said, and they all stared again. "Look, am I part of this or not?"

"Of course you are, dear," Victoria said. "Alec's just not used to hearing women say no in a bedroom."

"Aunt Vic—" Alec said, and Dennie cut him off.

"I met with Bond this afternoon," she said. "He likes me. He thinks I'm a gold digger out to get Alec's money. He'll believe me if I tell him I'm going for the house too." She looked up at Alec. "And it'll be a lot easier for me to confuse him than it would be for you. He's not going to be staring down your shirt."

Alec glared at her. "He's not going to be staring down yours either."

"Yes, he is," Harry said, and when Alec transferred his glare over, Harry shrugged and said, "She's right. She's our best bet."

"You had to wear that dress, didn't you?" Alec said bitterly.

Dennie nodded. "This dress clouds men's minds."

"Well, it's certainly working on Alec," Victoria said, and Alec gave up.

"Call him," he told Dennie, and when there was no answer in Bond's room, he said, "We'll have to try the bar. Get the wire, Harry."

"Which I will tape on her," Victoria said to Alec.

"Fine," Alec said, and thought, *But I'll take it off her.*

Alec found Bond in the bar without letting Bond see him, and ten minutes later, Dennie sat down a few seats away and waited for Bond to spot her.

It didn't take long.

"Dennie!" He slid onto the stool next to her. "Where's Alec?"

"He went up to bed," Dennie said sadly. "He likes to get plenty of rest. He sleeps a lot. And he's so awfully disappointed about not being able to get the house." She peered up at him woefully through her lashes. "I am too. I know it's money-grubbing of me, but I really want that house too."

"Aw, honey," Bond said, and slipped his arm around her.

Dennie leaned on him a little and looked up at him, her eyes huge with sorrow. "I don't want to marry Alec if all he owns is a bunch of land. He might never build a house. Men change their minds sometimes, you know?"

"Only the rotten ones," Bond said nobly, and Dennie refrained from rolling her eyes and went back to gold digging.

"I wanted to look out my bedroom window and see the ocean," she said, her breath catching on a little sob. "Just like a rich person. And now I never will."

Bond patted her shoulder, letting his hand slide a little as he patted. "Why, honey, you can do that if your Alec buys the property. He's crazy about you. He'll build you that house. Now you cheer up. Here let me get you another drink." Bond signaled the bartender without letting go of Dennie.

In the back room, Alec shook his head. "She's overplaying it."

"He thinks she's drunk," Harry said. "She's doing okay."

"Shhhh," Victoria said.

Dennie sipped her drink and tried to ignore the way Bond's arm was slipping down her back. She pantomimed fighting back another loud sob. "I just wanted to lie there in my bed and listen to the ocean pounding and pounding. You know? Just like it was pounding on my body."

"Really?" Bond said, stopping with his drink halfway to his mouth.

"Really," Dennie breathed.

* * *

In the back room, Alec said, "Oh, come on," and Harry and Victoria both shushed him.

Dennie looked deep into Bond's eyes and dropped her voice to confide in him. "I sleep naked, you know? In the nude. Totally. And I could just feel the way those ocean breezes would just kind of *stroke* all over my skin, you know?" She ran her hand lightly down her arm. "Stroking and stroking."

"Stroking," Bond said, moving his hand up and down her waist.

"Stroking," Dennie said. "And the way my heart would just pound with the surf. Stroking and pounding. You know?"

"Yes," Bond said. "I know." His hand crept around her rib cage to settle tentatively under her breast.

"In fact, just thinking about it makes my heart pound," Dennie said. "Here." She pulled his arm from around her, curled his hand into a fist, and pressed it against the swell of her left breast. "Can't you hear it pounding? Can't you feel it?"

"God, yes," Bond said, his voice suddenly husky.

* * *

In the back room, Alec glared at the recorder. "What is she doing? What does she mean, can he *feel* it?"

"Quiet," Harry said.

"You know, she's very good at this," Victoria said.

"The hell she is," Alec said, and then winced when Victoria raised her eyebrows at him. "Sorry, Aunt Vic."

Bond was practically breathing down her cleavage, and it was taking all Dennie's strength to keep his fingers curled tightly in her fist. "I can feel it too," she said, breathing deeply against him. Then she shoved his hand away and turned her back to him. "But it'll never happen now. There's no house. No surf. No pounding. He'll never build it."

"Wait." Bond put his hand on her shoulder. "Wait. Maybe there's something I could do—"

Dennie swung around to him again and

pressed against him. "Could you? Oh, could you? I would be so grateful. So terribly, terribly grateful. This is just so important to me. I mean, having my own house and the pounding and all." She wet her lips and cast a glance around the bar before she turned back to him, putting her hand on his knee and dropping her voice. "You see, Alec is a dear, dear, *dear* man, and I do love him, I do, but sometimes he's not . . . well . . ."

"What?" Alec said in the back room.

What?" Bond said at the bar.

"Well," Dennie said, letting her voice rise. She put up her hand between them, as if to stop him from interrupting. "Now I don't want you to get the wrong idea, because Alec is a dear, dear man and I just love him to pieces, but he works so hard at making all that lovely money that sometimes, well, sometimes he's just a little . . ." She let her hand flop over to dangle limply from her wrist. "If you know what I mean."

* * *

"What does she mean?" Alec said, scowling.

"I know what you mean," Bond said.

"A little uninterested," Dennie finished.

"I'm going to kill her," Alec said. He heard Harry snort, and he looked down. Harry was laughing.

"I like this woman," Victoria said.

"That's it," Alec said, and started for the door.

"Not yet," Harry said, and Alec stopped at the door.

"Oh, hell!" he said, audibly grinding his teeth and stomped back to the recorder.

"That's a shame about Alec," Bond said, leaning closer until he was plastered against Dennie. "Is there anything I could do to . . . help?"

"I wish there were," Dennie said, trying to keep from falling off her stool. He was practically in her cleavage, and his weight was making her slide backward. "But since you can't guarantee us a house . . ."

"Well, I *might* be able to do that," Bond said, moving closer and breathing heavier.

"I'll be damned," Harry said.

"I don't believe it," Alec said. "He fell for that line?"

"I don't suppose the line is all he fell for," Victoria said. "That red dress is probably doing some of the talking."

Alec glared at her. "Have we got enough yet?"

Bond's arm was back around Dennie now, his hand creeping up to her breast. "You're wonderful," Dennie said to him. "I just don't know how to thank you enough."

"Well, I think we could find a way," Bond said. "You know I've got to make a few phone calls on this, since it's such a special deal, just for you. And we don't want anybody else to know that you're getting . . . well, something extra." He leered at her as his hand moved over her breast, and Dennie fought back the urge to kick him. "Why don't you just come back to my room with me and"—he ran his free hand up her waist—"and we'll talk about it. And then maybe I'll make those calls."

"Oh, *Brian,*" Dennie said.

"Oh, *brother,*" Alec said. "That's it. She's out of there." He was out the door before Harry could stop him.

"Just the two of us," Bond was saying into her neck. "To cement the deal."

Dennie tried to figure out how to slide away from him without seeming to. One of his arms was wrapped around her, his hand clamped on her breast, the other was sliding down her waist to her hip, and his head was buried in her neck where he was doing something wet with his tongue that even Walter would have been ashamed of.

She had to distract him. "Well, I'll certainly

never forget that kiss you gave me," she began as she tried to disentangle herself, "but—"

Immediately, Bond fastened his mouth on hers and did a repeat of the oyster kiss with extra saliva.

Dennie wrenched her mouth away, trying not to spit. "But I think Alec would just be real upset if we —"

Bond pulled her back to him. "Alec's asleep." He bent to her neck again, and Dennie looked past his head to the doorway.

Alec was there, glaring at her.

"Brian, stop it," she said, trying to shove him away. "He's here."

"What?" Bond's head came up groggily. "Who?"

"Alec!" Dennie shoved him harder. "He's over there in the doorway. I don't think he's seen us yet, but—"

Bond let go of her so fast, she almost fell off the stool.

Chapter 8

❧

"Dennie!" Alec came over wearing his best doofus grin. "Honey, I've been looking all over for you."

"Well, I've been right here. And Alec . . ." Dennie leaned toward him as he took the stool on the other side of her. "Brian says he thinks he can guarantee us a house, after all."

"Uh . . ." Bond frowned. "I said maybe . . ."

Alec put his arm around her and pulled her closer to him. "Brian, that's terrific. If you can guarantee my little girl a house, you've got a deal."

"Well—" Bond said.

"And we'd be so grateful," Dennie said, smiling

at him. "*I'd* be so grateful. On account of the pounding, you know? And the stroking."

"Right," Bond said, and Alec pinched her to let her know she was going too far. "Of course, I'll have to make a few calls . . ."

"Great!" Alec slid off his stool and pulled Dennie with him. "Dennie and I'll go up to my room and wait. You've got the number?"

"Uh, yeah, but—"

"Oh, Brian," Dennie said, and pulled away from Alec to throw her arms around him. "I just can't tell you how *warm* this makes me feel."

Bond looked down at her, suddenly breathing a lot heavier, and Alec grabbed her arm. "She is a grateful little thing," he told Bond as he pulled her away and stepped in front of her. He let his voice drop when she was behind him. "Why when I gave her that diamond, you know what she did?"

"What?" Bond said.

"Well." Alec wiggled his eyebrows. "All I can tell you is that we used up an industrial-size can of hot fudge and four cans of whipped cream. The maid never did get that mattress clean."

"Alec!" Dennie said, pretending to be scandalized. Then she winked at Bond.

"Whipped cream," Bond said. "Damn."

Alec stepped even closer and dropped his voice another notch. "Imagine what she'll do for a house, huh?" He dug his elbow sharply into Bond's ribs, laughing his snort laugh, and Bond laughed along after he got his breath back from the dig. "Now you call us when you're done phoning your people."

"You sure I won't be interrupting anything?" Bond asked archly.

"Hey, what could be more important than this?" Alec said, and out of the corner of his eye he saw Dennie let her hand flop over limply at her wrist.

Bond slapped him on the back. "Can't think of a thing."

"Great," Alec said, and towed Dennie toward the door. "What in the hell were you doing?" he asked her when the elevator doors were closed behind them.

"What do you mean?" Dennie said. "I did exactly what you told me to do. I convinced him to guarantee us the house."

"You were supposed to *cry* on him," Alec said. "Not have sex with him in the bar."

Dennie rolled her eyes at him. "Alec, men don't do things for women who cry on them. They do things for women they think they're going to get into bed." She crossed her arms and leaned back against the wall of the elevator. "You know that. You're just jealous."

"Jealous? Me? Jealous? Don't flatter yourself." Alec jammed his hands in his pockets and leaned against the opposite wall. "Do not flatter yourself."

"Is Harry upset with me?" Dennie asked.

"Harry thinks you should be in the movies," Alec snarled.

"Is Victoria upset?"

"She's going to nominate you for woman of the year."

"Well, see." Dennie shrugged. "The only one who's upset is you. And the only reason you'd have to be upset—"

The elevator doors opened, and Alec stormed out.

"—is because you're jealous." Dennie spread her hands out. "It's obvious." Then she let both hands go limp at the wrist as the elevator doors began to close.

Alec stuck his hand in the doors to hold them open. "Very funny. You're getting off here, too, dummy."

"Not with you in this mood." Dennie punched the button for her floor. "You can handle it from here."

"Oh, no." Alec shoved the doors open and yanked her out into the hall.

"Hey!" she said.

"If he asks to talk to you, you're going to be there." Alec propelled her down the hall in front of him. He unlocked the door to his room and motioned her inside. "Strictly business."

"It better be," Dennie said, and went in.

The first thing Dennie did was wash her neck off, rinse her mouth out, and remove the wire.

"Is it possible for spit to be corrosive?" she asked Alec, as she came out of the bathroom. "I think I'm breaking out in hives from him."

"It's your own fault." Alec was stretched out on

the bed, his hands behind his head, and he looked better than any man had a right to. His shoulders alone were enough to make a woman dizzy. "You were the one who leaned over and asked him to pound you," Alec said.

"I can't believe he fell for that." Dennie sat on the edge of the bed and kicked off her shoes, trying to think of other things besides jumping Alec. The thought was futile; sometime in the afternoon, she'd definitely decided to jump him, and not even the nauseating Bond had changed her mind. "I mean, while I was saying all that stuff, it sounded stupid, but he just ate it up." She rolled her eyes at him. "Men," she said, and thought, *Jump me*.

"Hey, wait a minute." Alec sat up. "I'm a man. I thought it was stupid."

"Yes, well, we all know your problem with pounding." Dennie let her hand flop over at the wrist.

"Stop that." Alec grabbed her wrist and held her tight, and Dennie held her breath. "That makes me nervous."

"Well, you have many other fine qualities." Dennie batted her eyes at him. "Some women aren't interested in erections. I'm not one of them, but I'm sure someday you'll find a lovely girl—"

"If you're looking for an erection, I'm pretty damn sure Bond has one right now." Alec reached for the phone with his other hand. "I could call him—"

"Don't even joke about it." Dennie stuck her chin out and leaned a little closer. "I'll never French-kiss again as it is. The thought of him naked and throbbing could put me off sex forever." She smiled at him, her shoulder almost touching his. "Then you and I would be *perfect* for each other."

"That's it." Alec pulled her to him, rolling over to pin her beneath him on the bed, and Dennie rolled with him, laughing as he landed on top of her, his weight finally relieving her need to touch him while it kicked that need into high gear. She wrapped her arms around his neck and pulled him closer as she arched into him, and he stopped. "Hello?" he said. "I just attacked you. You planning on fighting back?"

"Why would I fight back?" Dennie whispered, moving against him. "The only reason that I sat on your bed was so you'd grab me." She smiled up at him and saw his eyes go dark. He took a deep breath, and she slid against him again, running her hands hard down his back as she said, "I was hoping you could cure my new aversion to French-kissing."

"It'll be a sacrifice," he said, and licked into her mouth while his hips bore down on hers. Dennie closed her eyes and shuddered under him, wrapping her legs around him while she sucked his tongue into her. Alec rocked against her, and she yanked his shirt from the back of his pants so she could rake her nails down his naked back, loving the way he tensed under her hands. She felt his hand pull at the neck of her dress and then roughly slide the purple lace from her breast, and then his mouth was on her throat and then on her breast, and she pulled his head hard against her while he sucked and rocked her into more heat than she'd ever known possible.

When the phone rang, he didn't hear it at first, for which she was achingly glad. Then it rang again and he looked up. "Oh, hell," he said, and kissed her breast, and then her neck, and then her mouth, hard and deep, before he pulled back from her. The phone rang again. "It's Bond."

Not now, Dennie thought but she caught her breath and said, "Answer it. I'll still be here. Finish the job."

"I'm getting tired of the job," Alec said, but he kissed her again and then rolled off her to sit on the side of the bed and pick up the phone. "Brian? What's the good word?"

Dennie sat up behind him, listening to him babble to Bond like a moron while he set his trap, and she slowed her breathing to normal. Alec was amazing. She pulled her dress over her head and threw it on the floor in front of him, pleased to hear him stutter a little into the phone as he saw it fall. She pressed against his back, and she felt his muscles tense under her weight and the scrape of the lace of her bra against his skin. Then she reached around him and unbuttoned his shirt, feeling how hard the muscles in his back were against her aching breasts while her fingers trailed down his chest, tangling in his hair. She stripped off his shirt when she had it unbuttoned. Alec never stopped talking to Bond, but he helped her by pulling his hands out of the sleeves. His hands were shaking, and she was glad because hers were too. She began to kiss her way down his vertebrae, tickling each one with her tongue as she went. By the time she reached his waistband, every muscle in his back stood out in sharp relief.

"That's just great, Brian," Alec was saying. Dennie slid her hands around his waist to the button on his waistband and then slowly slid his zipper down. Alec caught her hand before she could do more, pressing her to him, and he was so hard that she was breathless herself for a moment, stunned at the thought of him that hard inside her. She bit his shoulder, and then licked the bite, and then moved up his neck to his ear.

"You've got the contract ready now?" Alec said. "With the house guarantee?" He turned to look at her, running his hand up her side to her breast. She closed her eyes as his thumb stroked across the lace, and his palm pressed hard against her. "Dennie's thrilled," Alec told Bond. "You should see her face. Of course, I'll meet you in the bar. Fifteen minutes? You got it."

He hung up the phone and then before Dennie

had even registered what he'd done, he'd rolled to pin her underneath him again on the bed. "*God, you feel good,*" he said against her neck as his hands scooped under her and pulled her hips against his. "I'm never answering the phone without you again."

"Fifteen minutes?" Dennie wrapped her legs around him, trying to pull that lovely hardness as close as possible. "Fifteen minutes?" She dug her fingernails into his shoulders as he pulsed against her in response. "You're going to leave me like this?"

"No," Alec said. "He's going to wait." He slid her bra straps down over her shoulders, and when her swollen breasts were free, he caught his breath and drew his finger lightly over the slope of one, and then looked into her eyes. "You are so beautiful," he told her, and moved his hand gently to cup the naked fullness of her breast.

She was so hot, his hand felt cool against her and that made her even crazier. Her breath quickened as he brushed his fingers across her. "Please," she whispered, and then he bent to ease the heat by taking her breast in his mouth.

Dennie closed her eyes and moaned and gave

up sanity, moving against him while they both shoved clothing from each other with shaking hands until they were naked and slick with each other's sweat, tasting each other with heat and need, drunk on the salty sweetness of their bodies. Dennie raked her nails down his back, and moaned, "Now," and Alec yanked the drawer out of the bedside table, trying to find his condoms before they both lost their minds completely.

And then he was inside her, and the shock of him in her, the fullness of him, suddenly kicked her craving to a fever pitch and made her rock into him, jerking against him so hard that her hips lifted him as she pressed her head back into the pillows.

"Easy," he breathed. "Take it easy, love." He wrapped his arms around her and rolled onto his back, and Dennie felt herself slide down farther, harder onto him, felt the scream in her blood as every nerve she had expanded to meet him and everything inside her tightened and glowed hotter while he rocked and rocked into her over and over, until she didn't know what was pulse and what was Alec. Then it was too much, and she writhed and cried out and clawed at him but he only held her tighter, his hands holding her hips to him relentlessly while he licked inside her mouth, and then it all slammed into her, all the heat and the pressure and the tightness, and she screamed. Alec rolled her beneath him and kicked off the slam again, and Dennie let go and shuddered under him, over and over again, feeling every cell in her body empty into him in glorious response. In the aftershock of her climax, she felt him jerk against her, too, the way she had shuddered against him, and then he was beside her on the bed, holding her, and she felt empty without him.

He kissed her gently, and the kiss grew, neither of them willing to break it. When it did end, he let his lips roam her face, caressing her eyelids, her cheeks, and finally taking her mouth again, stroking his tongue gently into her. "I knew it would be like this for us," he whispered to her finally, and she said, "I know. I knew it too."

Half an hour later, when they were both drowsy and calm and achingly satisfied, Alec let go of her with more reluctance than he'd thought he was capable of. "I have to go," he said, and rolled out of bed and began to get dressed.

"What are you going to tell Bond?" Dennie asked sleepily. "About being late?"

"The truth." Alec grinned at her as he buttoned his shirt. She was tangled in the sheets, and her curls tumbled into her eyes, and she looked warm and satisfied and his. He wanted her again, and had to tell himself sternly, *Later.* "I'll tell him you were so grateful about the house that you grabbed me and ravished me before I could leave."

"That's not the truth," Dennie said, sinking deeper into the bed as she stretched and yawned. "You grabbed me."

Later, dammit, Alec told his body and said, "Close enough." He watched her for a minute, planning later, and then he said, "You're not thinking about doing anything dumb like leaving that bed, are you?"

"Nope." Dennie yawned again. "If I'm asleep when you get back, wake me up." She rolled onto her side and curled up, and her body was outlined by the sheet as it stretched over her curves.

"Count on it," Alec said, and went down to finish off Bond.

Half an hour later, he was back. Dennie heard him undress and then he crawled into bed beside her and wrapped himself around her from behind.

"That was quick," Dennie murmured, spooning herself into him.

"He said, 'Tomorrow,' " Alec said in her ear, and his breath made her shiver a little. "He wants you to be there when he signs the contract. You overdid it, dummy. He thinks you're going to be so grateful, he's going to get laid."

Dennie rolled a little so she was half on her back, her shoulder pressed against Alec's chest. "He told you this?"

"No, he told me the contract was so important to you that you'd want to see it signed." Alec kissed her shoulder. "You really sold him, I'll give you that."

"Thanks." Dennie nestled closer, loving his body even more now that she knew what it could do. "Got anything else you'd like to give me?"

"It's going to be like this from now on, isn't it?" Alec said sadly, as his hand moved up her body. "You're always going to be wanting something from me. All I'm going to hear is, 'What's in it for me?' Life will be hell."

"That's not what I said." Dennie rolled into him and let her own hand roam. "I'm pretty sure what I said was, 'Why aren't you in me?' At least, I think—"

Then Alec stopped her mouth with his, and they both forgot about Bond for the rest of the night.

The next morning, they had to remember him.

Dennie had slipped out of Alec's room at eight, wearing the red dress Alec was never going to forget and carrying the purple underwear that he was really never going to forget. "We're meeting Bond at ten," he'd called after her, and she'd waved the purple lace at him and closed the door behind her.

The room was a lot colder once she'd gone. What had been his plan? To talk her out of a life of crime, to talk her into moving to Chicago, and to talk her into bed with him. Only one to go. Not bad. Alec got up and headed for the shower, feeling very cheerful.

Two and a half hours later, he wasn't nearly as upbeat.

"I know they'll be here any minute," he told Bond.

Bond looked uneasy, clutching the contracts as if Alec were going to rip them from his hands, which Lord knew, Alec wanted to do. Bond had showed him the new clauses while they were waiting, and it was all there. Once they both signed it, he could arrest Bond and go back to seducing Dennie into moving to Chicago.

But first Dennie had to show up, dammit. Donald and Victoria would also be nice, and he didn't know where the hell Harry was, which was unusual to say the least, but Alec wasn't being greedy. All he really needed was Dennie. If Dennie were there, Bond would sign anything. "We were up late last night," he told Bond. "You have no idea how much Dennie wanted that house. That little girl can be very grateful."

Bond looked interested enough to loosen his

grip on the contracts a little. Alec remembered Dennie the night before. She hadn't been grateful but she had been amazing. The thought must have showed on his face because Bond leaned forward.

"She's probably still asleep," Alec said, getting up. "I'll just phone upstairs and check. Don't go away. She's bound to want to thank you personally."

"I'll be right here," Bond said. "You tell her I'm waiting for her," and Alec thought, *In your dreams, buddy,* and went to call Dennie and find out what the hell was going on.

Dennie had her own problems.

She'd hit the lobby a little past ten, knowing she was a few minutes behind and hurrying because of it. She'd showered and changed into a purple jersey dress that could be left unbuttoned at the top, a good idea since Bond was a sucker for cleavage and they wanted him as happy and as distracted as possible. After experimenting with three buttons undone, which made her look like a tramp, and two buttons, which made her look only trampish, she'd decided on three and then realized she was late. Self-conscious about her cleavage and guilty about being tardy, she'd almost run Baxter down when he came to stand in her path.

"Uh, Miss Banks?" he said, recovering and trotting beside her.

"Not now, Baxter," Dennie said. "I'm late for a meeting. Not with Janice Meredith. Go away."

"This is about Miss Meredith," Baxter said, breaking into a trot. "She seems to have called the police."

Dennie stopped in her tracks, and he overshot her and came back. "The police?" she said. "Why? I didn't go near her."

"Evidently you talked to a friend of hers and the friend called and there was an argument and she blames you." Baxter spit it all out in one breathless sentence, and Dennie thought, *Victoria, you were supposed to be tactful.*

"Okay," Dennie said. "We can handle this."

"I would really prefer you just left the hotel," Baxter said. "If you leave, I'm sure she won't pursue this."

"I can't leave." Dennie turned to go toward the bar. "I'm late for—"

She bumped into a guy in a dark suit, standing next to a really beautiful brunette.

"That's her," the brunette said. "She's in it with him."

"In what? With who?" Dennie looked from one to the other. "I have to meet somebody. Can this wait?"

"Who do you have to meet?" the guy in the suit asked, and Dennie said, "That is none of your business." She detoured around them and headed for the bar, but before she could get there, the man caught up with her and put his hand on her arm.

"I just need to ask you a few questions," he said. "I'm with the Riverbend police." He showed her his badge, and Dennie's heart clutched, but since the brunette wasn't Janice and the suit wasn't reading her the Miranda spiel, she told herself to calm down.

Dennie craned her neck to see inside the bar. Alec was sitting with Bond, checking his watch. "I tell you what," she said to the suit. "I have to go in there and talk to somebody, and you can stay out here and watch. Then I'll come back out here and answer any questions you want. I really do have to go. I'm late. It's only going to be about fifteen minutes." She smiled at him as winningly as she could, but he seemed unimpressed.

"What somebody?" the suit said.

"See the blond guy sitting in there at the table?" she said, and then realized that could be either Alec or Bond.

"I told you," the brunette said with a great deal of satisfaction.

"I think we'll go in there with you," the suit said.

Dennie could just imagine how Bond would feel if she showed up with two extra people, one of whom was a cop. She was pretty sure Bond would spot a cop. She was also pretty sure that Alec wouldn't be happy either.

"Look," she said. "I can explain—"

"Miss Banks?" someone said from behind her.

Dennie turned, and there was another suit. He bore a vague similarity to the other suit with her, and even more telling, he had Janice Meredith with him.

"This is going to be bad, isn't it?" Dennie said.

Chapter 9

∽❧

"That's her," Janice said, and Dennie said, "Wait a minute."

"Dennie Banks, you are under arrest for stalking," the second suit said, and the first suit said, "That too?"

"Tom?" The first suit squinted at the second one. "What are you doing here?"

"Arresting her for fraud," Tom said. "Stalking, too, huh?"

They seemed to be bonding, so Dennie tried to sidle away and signal Alec. If she'd ever needed to be rescued it was now. Unfortunately, the second suit took the sidle badly and handcuffed her.

"Hey!" Dennie said.

"You have the right to remain silent," the second suit said while Janice and the brunette smiled their satisfaction and Tom shook his head. "Stalking too. You really take risks, lady."

Dennie closed her eyes and thought fast.

"Isn't that Dennie?" Donald asked Victoria as they walked through the lobby on their way to the bar and Bond.

"What?" Victoria was irritated. They were half an hour late because Donald had insisted on proposing in the elevator. In a rare moment of flair, he'd punched the emergency stop button and refused to punch it again until she'd said yes. Only after thirty minutes of tactful refusal followed by blunt refusal followed by invective had Donald given up and let the elevator descend. Even now he seemed hopeful. There was probably something to being that dumb, Victoria decided. Anything that let you ignore reality with that much persistence had to be helpful.

"Do we *know* those people?" Donald said, the first signs of his own irritation showing.

Victoria followed his eyes. Dennie was with two men in suits and two women, and she didn't look good. Then one of the women turned, and Victoria said, "Oh, *hell*." It was Janice. And the last time Victoria had spoken to her, Janice had not been a happy woman.

One of the suits put handcuffs on Dennie, and Victoria took Donald's arm and swung him around before he could see. Dennie in handcuffs would definitely be something he would discuss with Bond.

"Why don't we go talk to Bond about the land?" she said smoothly, steering him toward the bar. "Then I'll go see about Dennie."

"I don't know, Victoria," Donald said. "Why would I want to buy the land if you're not going to be with me?"

Victoria hated herself for what she had to say next. "You give up too easily, Donald." He brightened, and she picked up their pace. "Now get in there and buy that land."

* * *

"Okay, hold it," Dennie said before the second suit had finished his recitation of all of the things she had a right to. She turned to Tom and the brunette. "I don't know what your deal is, but I'll get to you in a minute." Then she turned back to Janice. "But your deal I know, and you should be ashamed."

"*I* should be ashamed." Janice's brows snapped together. "You have been *pursuing* me—"

"I have left you alone and done everything in my power to reassure you," Dennie snapped back. "But that's not the point. The point is, talk is cheap, lady. You make big speeches about risking, and then you turn tail and run the minute the most important risk of your life is in front of you." Dennie shook her head. "I really *admired* you. One of the reasons I wanted that interview was because I wanted everybody to know how smart you were, about life and relationships, and how the end of a marriage doesn't mean it was a failure, and about everything else you know that I don't and that nobody else does, either, and I wanted to be the one to help you tell them. And then you pull this."

Janice didn't look convinced. "I'm not the one in trouble here," she told Dennie. "You're not going to fast-talk your way out of this."

"I'm talking truth." Dennie leaned forward. "And you are the one in trouble here. *I'm* the one who could help you out if you weren't shoving your head so far into the sand."

"Just get her out of here," Janice said to the second suit tiredly. "I just want her away from me."

Dennie's temper spurted. "Oh, and for the record, you remember that crack you hit me with in the elevator about reputable journalists not eavesdropping?"

Janice tried to level her with a glare. "I remember nothing about you."

"Well, you're a hypocrite on top of everything else," Dennie said, her voice rising as the second suit tried to tug her away. "Because I read about your first scoop, and you got it by overhearing two diplomats on a commuter train. You must have been something back then."

Suit Two tugged on her arm, and then someone caught her other arm and she swung around to face the new problem.

"Handcuffs," Alec said. "This is a good look for you, but more about that later." He smiled at the two suits. "Gentlemen, I sympathize with your impulses, but you're going to have to uncuff her. She's working for me, and you're screwing up a very nice party here."

Dennie craned to look over his shoulder. Victoria and Donald were talking to Bond, Victoria all but bending over the table to distract him. With Alec between her and Bond, there was a fair hope he hadn't noticed the handcuffs and the cops. But only a fair one unless they moved fast.

Tom was handing Alec back his identification when she turned to tell him to hurry up. "Well, this is interesting," he said to Alec. He gestured to the brunette. "This little lady has some information too."

Alec looked at the little lady appraisingly. "Hold on to her, will you?" he said to Tom. "I think we may have some information of our own."

"I want a deal," Sherée said.

* * *

Dennie sat down at the table in a flurry of purple jersey, praying the fourth button would hold or she'd get arrested again. "Sorry," she said to Bond. "We were up late last night."

Bond smiled back into her cleavage. "I heard. I bet that doesn't happen often."

Dennie heard Alec stir beside her and kicked him on the ankle to make him behave. "Only when I get a house," she said. "I am getting one, right?"

"Right." Bond tore his eyes from her breasts with great difficulty and shoved the contract across to Alec.

"*Great* deal," Alec enthused, and signed with a flourish.

Dennie took the contract and handed it to Bond, leaning closer as she did so. "I want to watch you sign it," she whispered.

He straightened a little and shot a smile around the room. Then the smile faded. Dennie followed the direction of his eyes and saw Sherée, somehow detached from Tom, walking as fast as she could toward the lobby doors.

"Brian?" Dennie said, and leaned closer. "Honey?"

He turned and looked directly into her cleavage. "I thought I saw somebody I knew," he said, his eyes moving from Dennie's breasts to Sherée's retreat and back to Dennie's breasts again.

Oh, hell, Dennie thought, and drew in as deep a breath as she could, filling her lungs all the way to her toes. The fourth button popped, and she said, "Whoops," and shoved the pen in Bond's hand. "Sign it, honey."

He signed.

"From now on, you wear turtlenecks," Alec said.

An hour later, Dennie's life was a little simpler. Bond had been taken downtown for further questioning—"Like the next fifteen years," Alec said—and Sherée had finished explaining her bolt—"I was so nervous, I just needed some fresh air"—and Donald was making his move on Victoria once more, which was vaguely amusing since this time it wasn't Dennie's trauma.

"How clever of you to trick this Bond fellow," Donald was saying to Victoria. "Although you really should have told me. I could have been a geat help."

"You were a great help, Donald," Victoria said, looking around for someone. "I'm going to miss you."

"Nonsense," Donald said. "I realize now that the argument we had in the elevator was because you were distracted by all of this. You'll marry me yet, you'll see."

"Actually, she probably won't," Alec said, coming to stand beside Dennie. "Aunt Vic is married to her career. Nice try, though, Mr. Compton. Best of luck in the future."

Dennie leaned against him a little, and his arm went around her. He'd rescued her, he'd been there when she'd fallen, just as he'd promised.

For some reason, Dennie wasn't as grateful about that as she thought she'd be.

"Nonsense," Donald was saying. "A woman like Victoria should be married."

"That's what I thought," Harry growled from behind him. "That's why I asked her."

Dennie felt Alec's arm drop away from her.

"Harry?" he said.

273

"If you think I'm going to ask for her hand in marriage from you," Harry snarled at him, "you're nuts."

"Let me get this straight." Alec looked from Harry to Vic and back again. "You weren't around for the arrest this morning, which is unheard of, and now you're marrying my aunt and moving to Columbus?"

"No," Harry said. "I'm marrying your aunt and going God knows where. Chicago is yours. I quit."

"You quit." Alec swallowed, and then he looked at Victoria. "You're going to take Harry onto a college campus with you."

"No, I quit too," Victoria said.

Dennie patted his shoulder. "Hang in there. Change is good for you."

"I thought that was trauma," Alec said.

"That too," Dennie said. "Say congratulations to your nice aunt and new uncle."

"Uncle *Harry*?" Alec said, and Harry said, "Oh, *hell*."

* * *

Another hour later and the lobby had emptied, Harry and Vic gone to catch a plane and Donald off to console himself with a drink and a sympathetic Sherée, who promised to tell him everything she'd done to save him when she'd turned state's evidence against Bond.

Alec was never happier to see people go in his life.

"I don't want another morning like this one," he said, putting his arm around Dennie and trying to steer her toward the elevators. "I think we should go upstairs to bed and start this day over."

"I can't." Dennie stood still, and Alec had to stop or lose her.

"Is this the Janice Meredith thing?" he asked. "Because I can fix that."

"I don't want you to fix it," Dennie said. "Remember that thing you said about catching me until I was ninety-six?"

"Yes," Alec said. "And I will."

"I don't want you to," Dennie said. "I want to catch myself. I need to know I can make it myself. Alone."

Alec felt cold. "I was with you until you got to the last word."

"Listen, all my life Patience was there for me." Dennie came closer to him until she was almost touching him, her eyes directly on his. "And then today you were there. But there was a tiny moment, only a couple of minutes, where I had to fight my own battle. And I liked it. I just never got a chance to finish it." She bit her lip. "I love you, Alec, but I have to do this first. I need to be on my own."

"How long?" Alec asked, and his voice cracked as he said it.

"I don't know," Dennie said. "Six months. A year. As long as it takes for me to know that I don't need you to save me. Then I can come back to you and just need you to love me."

He looked so unhappy that she almost relented, but just as she was about to give in, he stepped back. "Okay. How soon do you have to start?"

"Now," Dennie said, and he sighed and said, "I figured that. Janice Meredith?"

Dennie nodded. "She and the police are waiting for me in the manager's office. And you have to go downtown for the Bond thing anyway, and then you have a plane to catch. I heard Harry tell you so."

He said, "I can change the flight," and she shook her head.

"I need to get moving on this," she told him. "I'll call you when I get settled. I just need the time first."

"Right." Alec sighed and took a business card and a pen from his breast pocket. "This is my home phone," he said as he wrote, "and the business phone, fax, and e-mail are on the card. Call collect. And call often."

He sounded unhappy but resigned, and she took the card from him and said, "I'll call a lot." She stretched up and kissed him, and he caught her to him and changed the kiss from a good-bye into a promise, and she didn't ever want it to stop. "I have to go," she said when she finally pulled away, and he let her go, but then he called her name when she was halfway across the lobby.

"Button up," he said when she turned. "I don't think Janice Meredith is going to appreciate the effect of those three buttons the way I do."

Dennie laughed and buttoned up, and then she watched him walk toward the lobby doors and out of her life. *Just for a while,* she told herself, but there were no guarantees. Life was what you went after.

Armed with that thought, she walked into the manager's office and found Janice Meredith sitting there alone.

"I sent the police away," Janice said, still looking at Dennie as if she were roadkill. "But I'm still not giving you the interview."

Dennie put her hands on her hips. "I have a lot of excellent reasons why you should." *And I just put an excellent man on hold so I could tell you them,* she added silently. *So you're going to listen, lady.*

Janice relaxed a millimeter into her chair. "I thought you might. You have five minutes."

Dennie closed the door behind her and sat down, putting everything she could into her next sentence. "Do you know the story about Margaret Mead? Somebody asked her why her marriages had failed and she said . . ."

Chapter 10

ﬆ

Four months later, Alec Prentice sifted through the last box of documents from the Bond case as the August sun streamed through his office window. His office now, not Harry's. He was glad about that and not glad. He missed Harry snarling at him. He missed Harry ignoring him while pounding the computer. But mostly he missed Dennie.

She'd called every day—or he'd called her when she'd stayed in one place long enough to have a number—until last week when the calls had trickled down to three. Then this week, there hadn't been any at all. She was on the road again, no number for him to call, and the worst part was, this was the week she was deciding which job in New York she was going to take. She'd gotten three offers after the Meredith article had been published, two not-so-good ones and one very good one, which had seemed like a no-brainer to Alec but not to Dennie. There must have been something else.

Maybe she'd been trying to tell him they were finished. They'd spent only four weekends together. He hadn't even met Walter yet. You couldn't build a relationship on that. Well, Alec could, but evidently Dennie couldn't.

He checked the last of the documents and was beginning to unload everything from his desk back into the box when he noticed one more paper, stuck half under the folded bottom of the carton.

It was the fax Aunt Vic had sent him. "Four Fabulous Days! Three Glorious Nights!" *Oh, hell,* Alec thought. If he'd only known the damn thing was a prediction instead of a come-on, he wouldn't have . . .

The hell he wouldn't have.

All right, he needed Dennie and she thought

she didn't need him, but that was wrong. He'd just track her down and—

I have to do this on my own, she'd said. All right, he wouldn't track her down. He'd just sit tight and trust her on this. He loved her. She loved him. She'd come through.

Maybe.

He shoved the sorted papers off his desk into the box and punched the intercom for his secretary. "All this stuff can be filed, Kath," he told her. "Whenever you've got the time."

"I can do it now," she said cheerfully. "Also you have a call on one." Her voice grew cheerier. "It's Dennie."

Alec grabbed the phone, and all his altruistic plans went south. *"Where have you been?"*

"I've been busy," Dennie said lamely, but even lame, her voice was wonderful. She went on, her voice full of nerves. "A few things came up."

"A few things? *A few things?* You didn't call for *three days*." Alec leaned back in his desk chair and told himself to calm down. "You had me scared to death."

"Sorry," Dennie said, and her voice cracked.

Something was wrong. His pulse kicked up again. "Don't ever do that again. Now tell me what's wrong, and we'll fix it."

"Nothing's wrong, and I won't do it again." Dennie stopped, and Alec gave her as long as he could before he prompted her.

"So. Which job did you decide to take?"

"What?"

"Which job? You had three offers in New York, remember? Which one did you take?"

"Well, actually, none of them." Dennie swallowed again. "I sort of jumped."

Alec's heart sank. More job-hunting. Less Dennie. "None of them?"

"None of them. I didn't like New York." She hesitated. "You weren't there."

"Oh." Alec's heart rose again. So maybe she'd come to Chicago. He closed his eyes at the thought and started thinking of arguments to convince her. "Good decision."

"I thought so." Dennie's voice picked up a little more speed and a lot more confidence. "So since the *Trib* loved the article I sold *Chicago Magazine* on the database, I called them. I have an interview tomorrow."

"The *Trib*? The *Tribune*? The *Chicago Tribune*?"

"That's the one." Dennie sounded unnaturally breezy. "I see them tomorrow."

"Oh." *Don't yell, "Yahoo,"* Alec told himself. *That would be immature.* "So when are you getting in? Can I meet you at the airport?"

"Uh, no. I told you. I jumped." He could hear her swallowing over the phone. "I know we never discussed commitment or anything, and I should have talked to you about this, but I couldn't stand it anymore, and . . . I'm here, Alec. I know I should have called to see if you wanted—"

"You're *here*?" Alec stood up. "You're at O'Hare?"

"No, I really jumped," Dennie said. "Walter and I are here in the lobby of your building."

"My building?" He almost dropped the phone. *"This building?"*

"Right. This building," Dennie said. "But if you don't want . . ."

Alec dropped the phone and headed for the

door. He took the six flights of stairs at a run when the elevator turned out to be at somebody else's floor—somebody else who didn't have the rest of his life waiting in the lobby—and he hit the ground floor at a run, only to stop in the middle of the lobby, lost. She wasn't there.

Then his eyes reached the row of old phone booths in the back. She was biting her lip, leaning a little against the booth, wearing a sleeveless white dress with a big red belt cinched around her waist and dangling red earrings the size of half dollars. He absorbed it all—her lush red lips and glossy dark curls and the fullness of her body above and below the red belt and most of all her eyes, huge with apprehension—all of her hit him like a punch to the solar plexus.

He went to meet her using everything he had not to run to her.

"Alec," she said, and the crack in her voice was there beside him, not over a damned telephone wire, and she was there beside him, not half a continent away, and the lobby was full of people. He took her arm—she was warm and solid and right there with him and he lost his breath for a minute—and hauled her out the front door and around the corner of the building to a side street, and then he pulled her into his arms and kissed the breath out of both of them, falling into her the way he had ever since that first kiss by her hotel door.

"We have to do something about this distance thing," he said when they'd both come up for air and he had her plastered up against the building. "I'm not letting go of you again."

"You don't have to take care of me," Dennie said. "I mean, just because I'm moving here doesn't mean that I expect to move in with you or anything. I don't even know if you like dogs, and Walter's a deal breaker."

Alec looked down and saw a surly-looking Yorkie staring back at him. "I love dogs." He held her tighter, still not quite believing she was there. "I'm crazy about Walter already—" Then the rest of it hit him and he stepped back a little to get a good look at her face. "What do you mean, you're moving here? I mean, I know you're moving here because I'm not letting you go anywhere else, but you're planning on moving here? Even if you don't get the *Trib* job?"

"I've moved." Dennie smiled at him, the smile that always said, *I can do this, I think.* "I told you. I jumped. Everything I own is either at the airport or being shipped as soon as I give them an address. That's why Walter's here."

"You've moved," Alec said, dumbfounded.

"It's all right," Dennie said hastily. "I'm not taking anything for granted. If you don't want—"

Alec cut her off. "It takes three days to get a marriage license in Illinois. Can you stand living in sin for three days?"

"Yes," Dennie said.

Alec took a deep breath. "Will you marry me in three days?"

"Yes," Dennie said, and he pulled her back close and thought, *Thank God.*

"I didn't think I'd ever hear you say it," he said into her hair as he rocked her back and forth.

"I always knew you would," Dennie said against his chest, all her confidence back. "I just wasn't sure what you'd say when I said it."

"Then you haven't been paying attention." He pulled back again so he could look at her. "Listen, as long as I'm on a roll, can I smear you with hot fudge and whipped cream on our honeymoon? I never did get to do that."

"Yes," Dennie said, beaming at him in relief. "You can smear me with hot fudge and whipped cream until you're a hundred. I love you. I couldn't stand being without you."

Walter barked and Dennie looked down. "You have to love him too, Walter. He's a deal breaker."

Walter sighed and laid down with his head on Alec's shoe.

Dennie looked back at Alec. "We're all going to live happily ever after," she told him. "Trust me on this."

And Alec said, "I do."

Two weeks later and twelve hundred miles away, Victoria picked up the mail at the end of the dusty dirt drive that led back into the sliver of undevelopable beachfront property she and Harry had bought from Bond after all. They'd gone down to look at it on their honeymoon, just to see what all the fuss had been over, and the sheer raw beauty of the place had left them standing in the middle of nowhere, staring at each other.

"He should have had pictures," Harry had said, looking around before he grinned at her. "The dumb cluck didn't know what he had."

"Can he sell land from prison?" Victoria asked, and Harry said, "Are you out of your mind?" Shortly after that, Bond found himself a lot richer, although not as rich as he'd hoped since Harry insisted on giving him a fair market price. Also he was still in prison and would be for a while, Sherée having proved very helpful at the end.

Victoria stopped halfway down the road and savored the birds and the smell of the ocean before she picked up speed. By the time she was up the gangplank on the *Victoria,* she was calling Harry's name.

"I'm up here," he called from the top deck. "It's a houseboat, Vic. I can't go far enough that you need to yell."

"I like yelling your name," she said, climbing the last stair to the roof. "Also we have mail." She tossed it in his lap, and he tipped his hat back and grinned at her. *God, I'm lucky,* she thought, and then, just to make him crazy, she said, "Donald wrote."

Harry scowled. "That idiot. Didn't you tell him you were married?"

"Yes." Victoria settled into her chair next to him and looked out over the water. "He wants to know where to buy a houseboat. Sherée is tired of Belize because there's nowhere to shop, and she heard we're living on this darling boat and she wants one."

"Tell me they are not docking next door," Harry said.

"Harry, we own next door," Victoria told him. "Also, both Donald and Sherée have the attention span of gnats. By the time they're back in the States, they'll want something else. They sound happy, and that's all that matters." She snuggled down in her chair and lifted her face to the sun. "Life is good," she said, and then she waved the letters she hadn't given him. "Alec also wrote. He and Dennie are ecstatic. Oh, and they're coming down next week on their honeymoon. They're bringing Walter."

"What?" Harry reached for Alec's letter. "Who's going to watch the database?"

"Harry," Victoria said warningly, holding the letter out of his reach, and he grinned.

"Right," he said. "No more database. I'll just have to make do with you."

"Life's hell," Victoria agreed, and stretched a little in the sun.

"Too much sun is bad for you," Harry said.

"There's nothing below but a bed," Victoria said.

"Like I said"—Harry stood and pulled her to her feet—"we'll just have to make do."

Sixty-two years it took me to get this, Victoria thought, laughing and following him down the stairs as he tugged on her hand. But when she got to the bedroom, she stopped. "I left Alec's letter up there," she told Harry, and ran back up the stairs.

She found it before it blew away, and as she picked it up she noticed there was something on the back. It was the invitation she'd faxed him five months before. "Thought you'd get a kick out of this," he'd written at the top. "And by the way, thanks for inviting me. I had a *great* time."

"Four fabulous days and three glorious nights." *More than that,* Victoria thought. *Fabulous days and glorious nights for the rest of my life.*

The wind blew up and took the letter from her, and she snatched at it to get it back but it blew out to sea.

It didn't matter. Its work was done anyway. The last line of the invitation had been right. Her life had never been the same. Victoria lifted her face to the sun one more time, and then went down to join Harry.

Life really was good.

Looking for more classic romance from
bestselling author Jennifer Crusie?
Then don't miss . . .

THE
CINDERELLA DEAL

%ə

By Jennifer Crusie

Now available from Bantam Books

Daisy Flattery is a free spirit with a soft spot for
strays and a weakness for a good story. Why else
would she agree to the outrageous charade offered
by her buttoned-down workaholic neighbor, Linc
Blaise? The history professor needs to have a fi-
ancée in order to capture his dream job, and Daisy
is game to play the role. But something funny happens on their way to the altar that changes everything. Now, with the midnight hour approaching,
will Daisy lose her prince, or will opposites not
only attract but live happily ever after?

Turn the page for a sneak peak inside. . .

Chapter 1

The storm raged dark outside, the light in the hallway flickered, and Lincoln Blaise cast a broad shadow over the mailboxes, but it didn't matter. He knew by heart what the card on the box above his said:

Daisy Flattery
Apartment 1B
Stories Told, Ideas Illuminated
Unreal but Not Untrue

Linc frowned at the card, positive it didn't belong on a mailbox in the dignified old house he shared with three other tenants. That was why he'd rented the apartment in the first place: It had dignity. Linc liked dignity the way he liked calm and control and quiet. It had taken him a long time to get all of those things into his life and into one apartment. Then he'd met his downstairs neighbor.

His frown deepened as he remembered the first time he'd seen Daisy Flattery in the flesh, practically hissing at him as he shooed a cat away from his rebuilt black Porsche, her dark, frizzy hair crackling around her face like lightning. Later sightings hadn't improved his first impression, and the memory of them didn't improve his mood now. She wore long dresses in electric colors, and since she was tall, they were very long, and she was always scowling at him, her heavy brows drawn together under that dumb blue velvet hat she wore pulled down around her ears even in the summer. She looked like somebody from *Little House on the Prairie* on acid, which was why he usually took care to ignore her.

But now, staring down at the card on her mailbox, appropriately backlit by the apocalyptic storm, he knew there was a possibility he might actually have to get to know her. And it was his own damn fault.

The thought gave him a headache, so he shoved his mail into his jacket pocket and went up the stairs to his apartment and his aspirin.

* * *

Downstairs, Daisy Flattery frowned too, and cocked her head to try to catch again the sound she'd heard. It had been something between a creaking door and a cat in trouble. She looked over at Liz to see if she was showing signs of life, but Liz was, as usual, a black velvet blob stretched out on the end table Daisy had rescued from a trash heap two streets over. The cat basked in the warmth from the cracked crystal lamp Daisy had found at Goodwill for a dollar. The three made a lovely picture, light and texture and color, silky fur and smooth wood and warm lamp glow. Unbelievably, fools had thrown away all three; sometimes the blindness of people just amazed Daisy.

"Hello?" The petite blonde across the chipped oak table from Daisy waved her hand. "You there? You have the gooniest look on your face."

"I thought I heard something," Daisy told her best friend. "Never mind. Where was I? Oh, yeah. I'm broke." She shrugged at Julia across from her. "Nothing new."

"Well, you're depressed about it. That's new." Julia took a sugar cookie from the plate in front of her and shoved the rest toward Daisy with one manicured hand, narrowly missing Daisy's stained glass lamp. The lamp was another find: blue, green, and yellow Tiffany pieces with a crack in one that had made it just possible for her to buy it. The crack had been the clincher for Daisy: With the crack, the lamp had a history, a story; it was real. Sort of like her hands, she tried to tell herself as she compared them to Julia's. Blunt, paint-stained, no two nails the same length. Interesting. Real.

Julia, as usual, had missed color and pattern completely and was still on words. "Also, you're the one who has to come up with the bucks for the feline senior cat chow. I should eat so good."

"Right." Daisy scrunched up her face. She hated thinking about money, which was probably why she hadn't had much for the past four years. "Maybe leaving teaching wasn't such a good idea."

Julia straightened so fast, Liz opened an eye again.

"Are you kidding? This *is* new. I can't believe you're doubting yourself." She leaned across the table to stare into Daisy's eyes. "Get a grip. Make some tea to go with these cookies. Tell me a story. Do something weird and unpractical so I'll know you're Daisy Flattery."

"Very funny." Daisy pushed her chair back and went to find tea bags and her beat-up copper teakettle. She was sure the tea bags were in one of the canisters on the shelf, but the kettle could be anywhere. She opened the bottom cupboard and started pawing through the pans, books, and paintbrushes that had somehow taken up house-keeping together.

"I'm not kidding." Julia followed her to the sink. "I've known you for twelve years, and this is the first time I've heard you say you can't do something."

Daisy was so outraged at the thought that she pulled her head out of the cupboard without giving herself enough clearance and smacked herself hard. "Ouch." She rubbed her head through her springy curls. "I'm not saying I can't make it as an artist." Daisy stuck her head back into the cabinet and shoved aside her cookie sheets long enough to find her teakettle and yank it out. "I believe in my-self. I just may have moved too fast." She got up and filled the kettle from the faucet.

"Well, it's not like you ever move slow." Julia took down canisters one by one, finally finding the tea in a brown and silver square can. "Why did you put the tea in the can that says 'cocoa'? Never mind. Constant Comment or Earl Grey?"

"Earl Grey." Daisy put the kettle on the stove and turned up the heat. "This is a serious moment, and I need a serious tea."

"Which is why I'm drinking Constant Comment." Julia waggled her long fingers inside the canister and fished out two tea bags. "I have no serious moments."

"Well, pretend you're having one for me." Daisy sighed, envying Julia's optimism. Of course, Julia hadn't quit a safe and solid teaching job to become a painter, or spent the past four years living on her savings until she didn't have any. Daisy felt her head pound. "Julia, I don't think I can do this anymore. I'm tired of scraping to pay my bills, and I'm tired of trying to sell my paintings to people who don't understand what I'm doing, and I'm tired—" She bit her lip. "I'm so tired of worrying about everything." That was the thing, really; she was worn down from the uncertainty. Like water on a rock; that was what the edge of poverty did to you.

"So what are you going to do?" Julia asked, but somewhere there was a faint sound, half screech and half meow, and Daisy cocked her head again instead of answering.

"I swear I hear a cat crying," she told Julia. "Listen. Do you hear anything?"

Julia paused and then shook her head. "Uh-uh. Your water's starting to boil. Maybe that's it."

Daisy took the kettle off while Julia took down two mismatched cups and saucers, plunking her Constant Comment tea bag in a Blue Willow cup and Daisy's Earl Grey in the bright orange Fiestaware. Daisy poured the hot water over the bags and said, "Pretty" as the tea color spread through the cups.

"Forget the pretty tea." Julia picked up her cup and carried it back to the table. "You're in crisis here. You're out of money and you can't sell your paintings. How's the storytelling going?"

"Budget cuts." Daisy sat down across from her with her own cup and saucer. "Most libraries can't afford me, and it's a slow time for bookstores, and forget schools entirely. They all say I'm very popular and they'll use me again as soon as possible, but in the meantime I'm out of luck."

"Okay." Julia crinkled her nose as she thought. "How else were you making money? Oh, the jewelry. What about the jewelry?"

Daisy winced with guilt. "That's selling, but Howard won't give me the money until the end of the month. And he owes me from the end of last month, but he's holding on to that too. It's not that much, about a hundred, but it would help." She knew she should go in and demand her jewelry money, but the thought of Howard sneering at her wasn't appealing. He looked so much like her father that it was like every summer she'd ever spent with him condensed into two minutes.

Julia frowned at her. "So how much do you need? To keep the wolf from the door, I mean."

Daisy sighed. "About a thousand. Last month's rent, this month's rent, and expenses. That would get me to when Howard pays and then maybe something else will turn up." That sounded pathetic, so she took a deep breath and started again. "The thing is, I quit so I could paint, but I'm spending all my time trying to support myself instead of concentrating on my work. I thought I'd have a show by now, but nobody understands what I'm doing. And even though I almost have enough paintings for a show, I'm not sure what I'm doing is right for who I am now anyway."

Julia sipped her tea. "Ouch. Hot. Blow on yours first. What do you mean, you're not sure what you're doing is right? I love your paintings. All those details."

"Well, that's it." Daisy shoved her tea away to lean closer. "I like the details too, but I've done them. I think I need to stretch, to try things that are harder for me, but I can't afford to.

I'm building my reputation on primitive narrative paintings; I can't suddenly become an abstract expressionist."

Julia made a face. "*That's* what you want to do?"

"No." Daisy shut her eyes, trying to see the paintings she wanted to do, paintings with the emotions in the brushstrokes instead of in the tiny painted details, thick slashes of paint instead of small, rich dots. "I need to work larger. I need—"

The mewling cry that had teased her earlier came again, louder. "That is definitely a cat," Daisy said, and went to open the window.

The wind exploded in and stirred Daisy's apartment into even more chaos than usual. Liz rolled to her feet and meowed her annoyance, but Daisy ignored her and leaned out into the storm.

Two bright eyes stared up at her from under the bush beneath her window.

"You stay right there," she told them, and ran for the apartment door.

"Daisy?" Julia called after her, but she let the door bang behind her and ran out into the rain. Whatever it was had vanished, and Daisy got down on her hands and knees in the mud to peer under the bush.

A kitten peered back, soaked and mangy and not at all happy to see her. Daisy reached for it and got clawed for her pains. "I'm rescuing you, dummy," she told it when she'd hauled it out from under the bush and it was squirming against her. "Stop fighting me."

Once inside, she wrapped the soaked little body in a dish towel while Julia and Liz looked at it with equal distaste.

"It looks like a rat," Julia said. "I can't believe it. You rescued a rat."

Liz hissed, and when Daisy toweled the kitten dry, it hissed too.

"It's a calico kitten." Daisy got down on her knees so she could go eye to eye with the towel-wrapped little animal on the table. "You're okay now."

The mottled kitten glared at her and screeched its meow with all the melody of a fingernail down a blackboard.

"Just what you needed. Another mouth to feed," Julia said, and the kitten screeched at her too. "And what a mouth it is." Julia shot a sympathetic look at Liz. "If you want to come live with me, I understand," she told the cat. "I know you're legally dead, but even you must draw the line at living with a rat."

Liz glared at the kitten one more time and then curled up under the light and went back to sleep.

"A kitten doesn't eat much," Daisy said, and went to get food. She found a can of tuna on the shelf over the stove, stuck behind her copy of Grimms' fairy tales, a jar of alizarin crimson acrylic paint, and her cinnamon. She took down the can and called back to Julia. "Want some tuna?"

"No. I just came over to bring you the cookies, and then I got distracted." Julia and the kitten looked at each other with equal distaste. "You know, this is not a happy rat."

"Stop it, Julia." Daisy dumped the tuna onto a china plate covered with violets, scooped a third of it into a half round of pita bread, and divided the remaining two-thirds between Liz's red cat dish and a yellow Fiestaware saucer. She took the dishes back to her round oak table, dropping Liz's red bowl in front of her as she went. Liz was so enthusiastic about the tuna, she sat up. Daisy put the yellow saucer in front of the kitten and stopped to admire the violets on her plate next to the complementary color of the Fiestaware. *Color and contrast,* she thought. *Clash. That's what life is about.*

"Daisy," Julia said. "I know you're going to freak when I say this, but I can loan you a thousand dollars. I want to loan you a thousand dollars. Please."

Daisy froze and then turned to face her friend.

Julia stood beside the table in the light from the stained glass lamp, looking fragile and cautious and sympathetic, and Daisy loved her for the offer as much as she was angry that the offer had been made. "No. I can make it."

Julia bit her lip. "Then let me buy a painting. You know how I feel about the Lizzie Borden painting. Let me—"

"Julia, you already own three of my paintings." Daisy turned back to the cat. "Enough charity already."

"It's not charity." Julia's voice was intense. "I bought those paintings because I loved them. And I—"

"No." Daisy picked up the plate with her pita on it. "Want some tuna? I can cut this in half."

"No." Julia sighed. "No, I have papers to grade." She shoved her chair under the table and looked at Daisy regretfully. "If you ever need my help, you know it's there."

"I know." Daisy sat down next to the kitten, trying to concentrate on it instead of on Julia's offer. "If you come across an easy way to make a thousand bucks, let me know."

Julia nodded. "I'll try to remember that." The kitten screeched again, and she retreated to the door. "Teach that cat to shut up, will you? Guthrie is not going to be amused if he finds out you're keeping a cat in his apartment building. The only reason Liz gets by is that she's ninety-eight percent potted plant."

Once Julia had gone, Daisy got down on her knees next to the table so she could look the kitten in the eye. "Look, I know we just met," she told the cat. "But trust me on this, you have to eat. I know you've had a rough childhood, but so did I, and I eat. Besides, from now on you're a Flattery cat. And Flatterys don't quit. Eat the tuna, and you can stay."

Daisy picked up a tiny piece of tuna and held it under the kitten's nose. The kitten licked the tuna and then took it carefully in its mouth.

"See?" Daisy scratched gently behind the kitten's ears. "Poor baby. You're just an orphan of the storm. Little Orphan Annie. But now you're with me."

Little Orphan Annie struggled farther out of the towel and began to eat, slowly at first and then ravenously. Daisy pushed the unruly fuzz of her hair back behind her ears as she watched the kitten, and then she began to eat her pita.

"You're going to have to lie low," she told the kitten. "I'm not allowed to have pets, so we'll have to hide you from the landlord. And from the guy upstairs too. Big dark-haired guy in a suit. No sense of humor. Flares his nostrils a lot. You can't miss him. He kicked Liz once. He looks like he has cats like you for breakfast."

The kitten finished the tuna and licked its chops, its orange and brown fur finally a little drier but still spiky.

"Maybe you're an omen." Daisy stroked her fingers lightly down the kitten's back while it moved on to cleaning the plate. "Maybe this means things will be better. Maybe . . ."